S0-ARO-615

The River's Edge

YA SEARS
Sears, Tina, author.
The river's edge

JAN 0 4 2017

Prais

"Such a 1   coming
of age story. Truly chilling and captivating." — Diane Les
Becquets, best-selling author of *Breaking Wild*

"In a voice reminiscent of Scout in *To Kill A Mockingbird*,
Tina Sears evokes striking physical and emotional
landscapes that are rife with danger and secrets. It's a
marvel to witness her characters navigate this world that
Sears has created for them." — Wiley Cash, New York
Times bestselling author of *A Land More Kind Than
Home* and *This Dark Road to Mercy,* William Morrow/
HarperCollinsPublishers

"Sears has written a hard-hitting coming of age novel
that pulls the curtain off of family secrets and shame. She
lovingly captures the innocence of the time, and then swiftly
and honestly shows the darker side of it." — Jo Knowles,
author of *Read Between the Lines*

"Tina Sears is a brave and compassionate writer with a vital
story to tell. I believe this will be a book with the power to
heal." — Mitch Wieland, author of *God's Dogs*

"Tina Sears tackles a tough subject, having written about the
thievery of innocence. If there was ever any doubt about the
need to tell about such a crime, it is dispelled in this lovely
coming of age story set in the 1970s." — Laurie Salzler,
author of *After a Time*

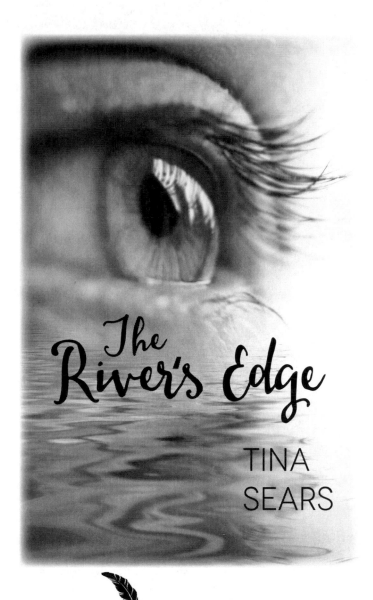

The
River's Edge

TINA
SEARS

BInk *Bink Books YA*
Bedazzled Ink Publishing Company • Fairfield, California

© 2016 Tina Sears

All rights reserved. No part of this publication may be
reproduced or transmitted in any means,
electronic or mechanical, without permission in
writing from the publisher.
This is a work of fiction. Names, characters, places, and
incidents are either products of the author's imagination or,
if real, are used fictitiously, and any resemblance to actual
persons, living or dead, events, or locales is entirely
coincidental.

ISBN 978-1-943837-40-3 paperback
ISBN 978-1-943837-41-0 epub
ISBN 978-1-943837-17-5 mobi

Cover Design
by

DESIGNS

Bink Books YA
a division of
Bedazzled Ink Publishing, LLC
Fairfield, California
http://www.bedazzledink.com

Dedicated to Katie Gnadt, who kept my head above water until I could swim again. She makes everything possible.

ACKNOWLEDGMENTS

Behind every novel is an author—the one who writes the words, but there are many behind the scene in guiding a story. Thanks to Sharon Killian, therapist extraordinaire, who set my truth on fire and chased the monsters away. I would also like to thank Jo Knowles, who helped me find my emotional truth, Wiley Cash, who helped me find my voice, and to Mitch Wieland, who set me in the right direction. Also thanks to Diane Les Becquets for encouraging me to be brave and the rest of the MFA writing community of Southern New Hampshire University. Special thanks to C.A. Casey and Claudia Wilde for their dedication to literary fiction that celebrates the unique and under-represented voices of women. Thank you to my first readers, Jackee Alston and Rebekah Aidukaitis, and to my sisters Lepha Sears and Becki Carlysle for shared stories.

CHAPTER ONE
BAPTISM

WHEN MY DAD left, Mom said he would come back to us, but I said I would believe it when I saw the whites of his eyes. I knew my dad was as reliable as a fart in a windstorm. He was a good dad when he was around, but he travelled a lot for his job. He would always bring me some sort of special gift when he returned. Something good, too. Not like some old crappy prize you get in a Cracker Jack box. One time he gave me a pen that had four different color inks. It had black, red, blue, and purple. Purple! My favorite color. It wasn't a girlie pink or a boyish blue, it was a color that rebelled.

I immediately grabbed my diary so I could write my life down in purple ink. Somehow it seemed that purple would make what I wrote down more exciting, like I was writing a Broadway musical.

But I guess he took one trip too many because he never showed up after the last one. That was nine months ago. After that, it seemed like a sadness fell over my mother that she never could shake. I was different. He disappeared right out of my life like a cruel magic trick and I didn't know how to bring him back, so I learned how to live without him, how to block my heart.

After he left it didn't seem appropriate to write in purple ink anymore, so I just wrote in black and blue because that's how I felt inside, all bruised up. When I really wanted to spill my guts, I wrote in red. So when Mom told me that I had to spend the summer with my relatives in Ohio, my diary looked more like a bloody crime scene than a field of lavender.

The first month after my dad left, Mom would jump when the telephone rang and answer it on the first ring, hoping it was him. But it never was. As time passed, she gave up answering the phone altogether because no one ever called except bill collectors. Lately when she smiled, she had a stare that looked far beyond me. The darkness that sometimes strangled her for days at a time had taken a stronger hold of her, and now she was sending me away for the summer because of it. Of course she didn't say it was because of that, but I knew. I knew deep down in my heart and I was afraid for her. I was afraid for myself.

One of my earliest memories of my parents together was at our house. We were in the front yard sitting on a blanket, having a picnic. My mom sang to me while she brushed my hair, and I blew dandelion puffs at my dad. But that was a long time ago, and I knew he was gone for good.

Now, as Mom backed out of the driveway, I took one last look at our house. It was no longer a home, but an empty, sad place.

"I don't understand why I have to spend the whole summer away," I said to Mom as we hit the road. "I won't get to hang out with my friends." I said *friends* but Lisa was my only friend. We were The Loners and didn't fit in with the cool people.

"Plus, I won't be able to swim on the team."

"They have a pool. Besides, this is a good year for you to visit your cousins. On the Fourth of July, there will be an extra special celebration because of the bicentennial."

"They have fireworks here, too, Mom." I was having what my mom called an "attitude problem."

"I don't know what's going to happen with your Dad being gone. I have to figure some things out." She paused. She rarely spoke about him to me anymore. "Besides, your aunt and uncle agreed to take care of you and that's final."

I sat in the passenger seat with my arms folded across my chest. The morning sun fought to find us through the tall trees as Mom navigated through the country. Shady areas were interrupted by splashes of sunlight, moving too quickly for my eyes to adjust. I closed them, but the sun was so bright, I could still see the strobe light affect through my eyelids.

I gave her The Silent Treatment. I had never been away from my mom and I wasn't looking forward to it now. But I also knew she was in a tight spot since Dad left, and that I should give her a break. I was what you call "conflicted" about the whole thing.

After an hour's drive, I saw a sign pass by quickly. "You are now leaving Virginia."

Virginia. Where I grew up and my family broke apart.

My mom saw the sign too and she reached over and touched my knee. "Come on, you can't be mad at me the whole trip. We still have a long way to go." She turned up the radio and started singing.

The memory of my mother singing to me as a child washed over me and loosened me up a bit. I loved her voice. I loved her. I could never stay mad at my mom for very long. I chimed in and after a chorus or two, we were like two kittens rolling in the grass again. When the Bee Gees came on the radio, we started to sing about mending our own broken hearts. Each sharp note cutting through me as I sang the words, asked the question, "Why does the sun keep on shining?"

The music filled up all the empty space between us. It felt good to sing out loud, my voice pushing up from my lungs. It was everything that I couldn't say and everything I wanted to say at the same time.

We sang and sang, and pretty soon, I wasn't just singing any more, I was yelling too, because I wanted to get rid of the bruises inside. And Mom started to sing-yell with me. We were singing like two crazy people. I think it helped her release some of the hurt she was feeling inside. I never felt closer to her.

After singing my guts out, I felt exhausted, so I laid my head against the warm window and fell asleep.

When I woke up, it felt like we had been in the car forever. We finally reached Cincinnati a few hours later and pulled off the interstate.

The two-way street started getting narrow as we headed into the country, and by the time we took a sharp right, the corn fields were closing in on us from both sides. The ears of corn bent their heads toward us as we passed by, bowing. There was barely enough room for one car, and if we encountered any oncoming traffic, we surely would be hugging the edge of the road to let them pass.

The sign that governed the entrance to the camp greeted us. It read, "Shady Grove" in big, hand-painted letters, and in smaller letters beneath it, "Private." We followed the one way dirt road with cottages on either side of us. Most had screened-in porches with cheerful outdoor lights strung along the top of them.

Two blocks later we reached Uncle Butch's cottage. It was wooden like the rest of them, and the white paint was chipping. It looked like all the other cottages in the place. They were small, one story cottages, each on a square of land with dirt roads cutting them into little fudge squares. The yard was only big enough for an old oak tree and a picnic table.

The cottage was my grandmother's, and both my mom and uncle inherited it when she passed on. They had grown up here during the summers in this place with few modern amenities. It had a washing machine but not a dryer, and you had to hang the wet clothes on a clothesline in the yard. When Uncle Butch married, he bought a house in Mount Adams, a subdivision just fifteen minutes away. Nevertheless, he never abandoned the childhood home he shared with my mother. His family moved into the cottage at the beginning of each summer and stayed until school started again in the fall.

There wasn't a driveway at Uncle Butch's cottage, so Mom pulled up in front of the screened-in porch as close as she could. When I opened my door it bumped up against the cottage and I had a hard time getting out of the car.

"They're here!" Aunt Lori's voice sang out.

My cousin Wendy greeted me with a big smile. "Hey, Chris."

"Hey," I said, a little nervous.

Although my cousin and I had written letters to each other, this was the first time I'd seen her since we moved to Virginia four years ago. I examined her for signs of maturity in her deep-dimpled cheeks and root-beer-colored eyes.

My aunt hugged my mother. "You made it! It's so good to see you again."

I reached in the trunk for my suitcase. I tried to hold my hand steady, forcing a smile.

My aunt walked up to me and hugged me tight, surprising me a little. Then she uncurled my knuckles from the handle of my suitcase. "Wendy, take this into the bedroom for Chris, would you, honey?"

Wendy took the suitcase and disappeared inside the cottage.

My aunt put her arm around my shoulders and scooped me up to her. My face was smashed up against her breast. "It's been so long since I've seen you. How are you doing?" She certainly was very enthusiastic.

She let me go so I could answer. "I'm doing okay."

"Just okay?" She hugged me tight again. "We're going to have to do something about that."

After she released me from her bear hug, she touched my mom's shoulder. "How are you feeling these days?"

"Oh," my mom sighed heavily, "I have good days and bad." Lately it seemed like all her days were bad, but I didn't say anything.

Wendy returned and leaned into me. "Come on, I want to show you something."

"Don't go near the river girls," my aunt called out to us as we left.

Wendy and I followed a dirt road that was muddy and full of pot holes. Then we crossed a grassy field until we reached a row of trees. We slipped between an opening of an overgrown path, barely visible from the cottage.

The underbrush bared its thorns as we ducked under them at the beginning of the path. We made our way downhill through scrub, across twisted roots, and into a section of pine trees. The pine scent was like perfume and the sprawling limbs spread over the top of us like a canopy.

The afternoon was alive with the smell of the Ohio River, of mud and honeysuckle so sweet I could taste it in my mouth. It reminded me of home, of how my mom taught me to pinch the flower and lick the nectar from the bulb. The sun-drenched river glowed like fire, and the expanse of water between us and the other side seemed like an eternity.

I stood beside Wendy on the edge of the river. "God! I can see forever," I panted, half winded from the walk, half breath-taken by the view. I saw something jutting out from the middle of the water.

"What's that?" I asked.

"Slippery Rock," my cousin whispered, as if uttering the name alone would cause something dreadful to happen.

"Does anyone ever swim out to it?" I asked.

"Too dangerous. Last time someone tried, the only thing that was found of her was that shoe," Wendy said, pointing to a tree right on the edge of the water. A muddy red tennis shoe was nailed to its enormous trunk, a reminder of the river's strength.

"No way. You're lying."

"No, I'm not."

"Have you ever tried?"

"Are you kidding? I don't even know how to swim."

"Maybe I can teach you how this summer," I said in a feeble attempt to connect with her.

"I don't know. Maybe." She shrugged.

My cousin and I were like two people standing on opposite sides of the river, recklessly leaning forward to speak to each other. The great distance between us made me homesick, and the summer was just beginning.

"Is this the river we're not supposed to be near?" I asked.

"Yeah, this is it."

"Then why are we here? You must love danger."

"Not really. This is where Julie and the gang hang out. They're the only ones because they're the popular kids and have claimed this spot as their own. Everyone else is afraid of them. But not me. I used to hang out with them."

"Used too? What happened?"

"Last year, the boys really started liking Julie, and she didn't want me around anymore. But I want back in to the group and this is my chance."

I followed Wendy over to a log and sat down next to her. We both had on tank tops, but mine was green to match my eyes.

"I like your hair like that," I said. "It's grown since the last time I saw you." We both had long blond hair but mine was pulled back in a ponytail and hers was hanging over her shoulder like angel hair pasta.

"Thanks. My mom said I could grow it out on account of my ears."

"What? That doesn't make sense."

"Yeah, my left ear is growing faster than my right and I'm lopsided. So I'm growing my hair longer to cover it up." Wendy stood up and pulled back her hair. "See?"

"You're not lopsided."

"I think I might have a brain tumor."

"What? That's crazy."

"My mom's sister died from a brain tumor and I have the same blood as her. It's possible."

"Sorry," I said, glad I wasn't related to her aunt.

I heard a girl's voice from the path. "Because I said so."

Wendy tapped my arm excitedly. "Julie's coming."

A few seconds later Julie appeared. Four boys stood behind her like loyal subjects.

She was the prettiest girl I had ever seen. Her fine blond-brown hair was pulled back into a ponytail, but the wisps at her hairline escaped, curling across the sides of her face. Her hair looked like the color of coffee with too much cream. Her eyebrows were two curves, like a child's drawing of a seagull in flight, and her lips seemed so full I thought it might take some effort to keep them closed. When she ran her tongue over them, the sun sparkled on the moisture.

She was everything I wanted to be and nothing that I was.

I took note of the boys behind her. One was skinny with freckles and a crewcut. The second was blond with piercing blue eyes. He was wearing cut-off jeans and a dirty white T-shirt. The third one wore a Reds baseball cap, and the forth had a wild cowlick that emphasized his round eyes.

"Get lost, punks. This is our territory," Julie said.

"We're allowed to be here," Wendy said. "It's a free country."

I wanted to tell that girl to shut up, but I swallowed my words and turned away, too shy to speak.

Nobody knew what to do next, but it felt like something big was about to happen. I could almost hear a drum roll.

Then the boy with the Reds baseball cap spoke. "Let them stay. There's no harm in it. Besides, you used to hang out with Wendy." Long dark hair spilled out recklessly under his cap. I liked him already.

"Dave? What's gotten into you?" Julie looked at him bug-eyed, mouth open, with her arms folded across her chest.

"Nothing. I just think there's no harm in it, that's all." His complexion was clear, especially compared to Freckles.

"But what about New Girl here?" Julie asked.

"We don't know her," Freckles said. He turned and spit in disapproval.

"We should still let them stay," Reds baseball guy said.

"Okay then." Julie puffed up and looked at us. "If you want to stay, you guys have to swim out to Slippery Rock."

I looked out at the rock. The distance to swim out to it seemed impossible. The sun made the river look like a thousand stars dancing on top of it. I heard birds chirping and I wished I could fly away home.

"Swim, swim, swim . . ." Julie started chanting.

A few seconds later, the boys chimed in. All but Reds. The chorus became louder. "Swim, swim, swim . . ."

I looked nervously at my cousin who was looking back at me, equally nervous. The chorus got louder. "Swim, swim, swim . . ."

"I can't swim," Wendy said above the chanting.

Julie gave me The Evil Eye. "Then you swim for the both of you, New Girl."

"Yeah, New Girl, you swim for the both of you," Freckles said, looking at the shoe nailed to the tree, then at me. "If you want to stay."

I was tired of this bull, tired of feeling left out, too shy to make very many friends. Tired of worrying about my mother all the time. I looked at Wendy with her lopsided ears, knowing that she was pinning all her hopes on me. I had nothing to lose so I studied the water as they continued chanting.

I walked to the riverbed and studied the black water. The river was swollen with rain and the constant up and down motion made it look like it was breathing. Wendy followed me.

"Don't do it," she said. We were far enough away from the group that I was sure they couldn't hear. I heard her say the words, but her eyes were saying something else entirely.

I looked away and kicked off my flip flops and walked to the river's edge and stopped when I felt something slimy under my foot. A dead fish stared up at me with its eye, unfocused and glazed over. Disgusted, I pushed further into the water, trying to shake the image.

I swam across the current diagonally toward Slippery Rock. The further I swam, the more I could feel the world changing. And not in a good way.

The water's flow carried me toward the rock and the cold made my muscles tighten. I thought of winning the first place ribbon in the butterfly stroke for my swim team last summer, and pride surged through me.

A few minutes later, my lungs began to burn. The current was going faster than I could motor across it. I swam harder, but my muscles tired and I let the current carry me. I had miscalculated. The force of the water pulled me under. It felt like giant hands were forcing me down and I couldn't break free. I wasn't going to make it. The water closed in around me. A glimmer of light filtered down through the murky water, then grew dark.

Under water, the river cut through me, pushing me farther from the rock. I had experience swimming in a pool where the water was clear and there was no current. But in this smelly, muddy water with the rushing current, I had no strategy to survive.

I kept sinking but just as I began to panic, my feet hit bottom. I pushed off with everything I had.

When I surfaced, I swam harder, the river threatening to pull me under again. Now I was past the rock and had to swim with twice as much effort against the flow. I struggled toward the rock but my wet clothes stuck to me, hindering my efforts. I tried to scream for help, but water rushed into my mouth. I know my scream drowned before it reached shore.

I heard a whisper inside of me. "Be brave." It was something my mother always said to me, especially after my dad left. I blocked out the pain from my burning muscles and swam toward Slippery Rock. I knew if I didn't make it to the rock, I didn't have a chance.

I filled my lungs with air, which helped me float. I put one arm out in front of the other and kicked my feet, closing the distance between me and the rock.

Finally the massive rock plunged up from the bottom like the wrinkled palm of a giant's hand, saving me from the river. The surface was covered with tiny hairs of moss dancing with the current, making it slippery. I couldn't get a grip. *Lord help me*. Then, as if in answer to my prayer, I felt a little crevice and pulled myself onto its surface.

Listening to the chattering rush of water across the rock, I looked over at the shore. Julie stood with her hands crossed against her chest. In contrast, my cousin was jumping up and down, screaming, and the boys were all waving me in. I could barely make out the group from my vantage point but I knew who was who from their clothing.

I raised one hand up in the air, triumphantly waving to the group while holding onto the rock for dear life with the other. I was stuck in the middle of the river, alone. Abandoned.

I forced a smile at the irony of it. I rested a few minutes, filling my lungs with deep breaths of air, letting my muscles relax.

"C'mon," the wind delivered. "C'mon, New Girl," Julie said, waving me in with the others.

I don't know why, but when I saw her waving me in, I wanted to scream at her for challenging me, but at the same time I wanted to prove to that stuck-up pretty bitch that I could do it. So I released my grip and jumped into the water with a battering jolt. My lungs emptied on impact. I lifted my arms out of the water while kicking my feet, sucking in a huge breath when I felt how cold the water was. I tried to swim toward the group, but the current took me down river. I closed my eyes and just kept swimming toward shore, praying that I would make it back alive.

Finally I reached land and collapsed on the riverbed, breathing frantically. Mud squished between my fingers as I tried to push myself up but my muscles were shaking. The wind brushed over my wet clothes, sending a chill down my back.

Everyone except Julie rushed over to me and helped me away from the riverbed back to the clearing. But I saw something in her expression like I had impressed her.

"I thought you were a goner!" Wendy said, smiling so wide her eyes almost disappeared above her cheeks.

I bent over and coughed up muddy water, happy that I survived.

"How did you do that?" Reds asked.

"Good job," Owl said.

I stood up and wiped my mouth with the back of my hand. Mom always told me that winning wasn't everything. I disagreed. At this moment, with everyone surrounding me, winning felt like *everything*.

Julie sauntered over to me, breaking through the group. "That was a stupid move, New Girl. I can't believe you did it."

"Well, you shouldn't make stupid challenges like that then," I said, staring into her eyes. Whatever her next move was, I knew I would be ready this time.

Julie sat down on a log and lit a cigarette in a practiced motion. "Wendy, what's your friend's name?"

"She's my cousin Chris."

Julie drew on her cigarette, sizing me up. "I'm Julie." Then she pointed to the blond guy. "And that's Tommy."

He smiled and nodded.

"Hi," I said, trying to be cool. I hope they didn't notice that my voice shot up a bit.

"That's Billy behind us," she said, pointing to Freckles. The sun shone high behind him, isolating each red hair on his head. He had a faint scar under his chin.

She raised her chin toward Reds. "That's Dave."

"And Max is behind those trees, bleeding the lizard." Reds pointed to the boy with round eyes, laughing.

Max was standing with his back to us, legs slightly parted. He zipped up and came over. He was twitchy, his head moving nervously from side to side, looking for what, I didn't know. He walked up to me, tucking something in his back pocket.

I pointed to each boy in the order they were introduced and said the nickname I had for them. "Hi Freckles, Reds, and Owl. I'm New Girl." Everyone laughed and I relaxed a little.

"Wendy?" Julie flipped out a cigarette from her pack and handed it to my cousin.

"Thanks."

I couldn't believe she took it. Freckles lit her cigarette, expertly cupping his hand to prevent the wind from blowing the flame out.

"Hey, New Girl. Want one?" Julie offered the pack to me.

In my brief hesitation, the boys stopped what they were doing and watched me. Wendy nodded her head urgently toward the cigarette, so I took one. I felt like it was a rite of passage, though I didn't know for what.

Freckles lit my cigarette, cupping his hand like he did for Wendy. The cigarette felt strange between my fingers. With my coordination skills, I was more than likely going to burn myself or start a fire than anything else.

I inhaled and coughed. It burned my throat and smoke got in my eyes. Why couldn't I ever pull off being cool?

"Is this your first time smoking?" Julie's question was laced with sarcasm.

"No." I coughed my way through another drag, feeling more and more light-headed.

Julie was the most comfortable smoking. She held the cigarette delicately between her fingers like a movie star. Then she pushed the smoke out through her full lips as if she was releasing a secret.

"I remember my first cigarette. I was ten." Owl swiped at the air, chasing a mosquito away.

"Oh, that's bull," Freckles said. "I gave you your first smoke last summer."

"That wasn't my first. My folks have always smoked. I snatched one when I was ten years old and smoked it in this very spot."

"I don't think that counts," Freckles said.

"Why not?" Owl asked.

"Because you took two hits and puked," Freckles said.

"I did not!"

"Yeah, you did, Puker," Freckles said. "I could tell you what you ate for lunch that day—pepperoni pizza. The pepperoni was still whole!"

"He's a puker," Tommy said, pointing to Owl.

"Gross," Reds said.

"Am not. Shut up." Owl pulled out a squirt gun he'd been hiding in the back of his shorts and pointed it at Freckles.

"Oh, I'm afraid. It's a squirt gun," Freckles said sarcastically. He put both hands to his mouth pretending to bite his nails.

"Stop it, or I'll shoot."

"Oh, I'm scared." Freckles laughed and looked at the guys for approval.

The first blast from the squirt gun landed on Freckles' forehead. Then again and again, until his face was totally wet. Freckles tried to block the barrage of squirts with his forearm but it was useless.

His mood darkened. "Stop it, dork. I mean it."

We all laughed, watching Owl unload the squirt gun until it was empty.

"You stupid jerk." Freckles cleared his eyes with the sleeve of his shirt. He looked confused and stuck his tongue out to a droplet above his lip. His faced soured. Then he swiped his forehead with his hand and brought it under his nose and sniffed. "Did you piss in that squirt gun?"

Owl's expression changed quickly from triumph to worry. Freckles lunged forward and grabbed Owl's shirt. The shirt ripped at the shoulder as he struggled to get free, but Freckles was taller and stronger, and he grabbed Owl around his waist and plunged him into a tree.

"It was only a joke," Owl said. His bottom lip was bleeding.

Freckles kept Owl's face against the bark while cursing, pushing him into the tree with each poisoned word, each movement making new scratches.

Owl gasped for air and spit blood out of his mouth.

"Do you give up? Huh?" Freckles pushed Owl's face harder into the bark.

Owl did what he could to nod his head, being that half of his face was smashed against the tree and hard to move.

I glanced at Wendy, not knowing what to do. She looked as nervous as I felt.

"Then say it!" Freckles yelled. "Say it!" He pushed again. "Say uncle!"

"Billy, that's enough. You're killing him!" Reds raced over and tried to pull them apart, but Freckles brought up his elbow and caught Reds in the face. The blow knocked his baseball cap off, bloodying his nose. Freckles looked back and seemed to realize what he had done. He released his strong hold on Owl and went over to Reds.

"Jeez, man, I'm sorry. I didn't mean to hurt you."

"Enough. Cut it out," Julie said. Everyone stopped what they were doing and looked at her. The queen had spoken.

I stared in disbelief. What had I gotten myself into? My heart raced. I never knew what to do or say in situations like this.

A while after the fight, we sat around on logs by the river's edge, talking. Well, *they* were talking, mostly about their plans for the summer. Since my future was so uncertain, I just kept quiet and listened. I don't know how much time had passed, but it was least an hour. I was almost dry when we heard a voice from the top of the path.

"Hey, dorks, time for dinner," a girl yelled. The sun forced beams of filtered light between the trees, causing me to squint toward her direction.

"We're not dorks," Wendy yelled back.

"Who's that?" Reds asked.

"Just my creepy little sister," Wendy said. She tapped me on the shoulder. "Come on, we better go."

I grabbed my flip flops and followed Wendy up the path.

"See you guys later," Wendy said halfway up the path.

"Yeah, see y'all later," I said.

"Y'all?" Julie said in her best southern accent, mocking me. "Where're you from, New Girl?"

"Virginia," I said over my shoulder as we hurried up the path to meet Paige.

"I'm not creepy," Paige said when we reached her. She was cute and had brown hair down to her shoulders with the same root-beer colored eyes as Wendy, but her complexion was darker than Wendy's.

"Are too," Wendy said.

"Hi, Paige."

"Hi, Chris," Paige said.

"You're so big. Last time I saw you, you were just a little bird," I said.

"Why are you all muddy?" Paige asked me.

"None of your business, dork," Wendy said.

"Better stop calling me names or else."

"Or else what?"

"Or else I'll tell Mom."

"Tell her what?"

"Oh, I don't know. That you were at the river." She held up two fingers as if offering a peace sign. After a moment, she grinned and put her fingers against her mouth and inhaled on a pretend cigarette.

"You brat," Wendy said, leaning into her face.

"It's okay." I pulled Wendy away from her. "She won't tell, will you, Paige?" I winked at her and put my arm around her shoulder. "I haven't seen you in ages. How old are you now?"

"I'm seven," Paige said, putting her arm around my waist. We walked arm and arm back to the cottage with Wendy following behind us.

As we neared the cottage, two kids exploded out of the neighbor's door, scaring me. They both had blond hair and looked like they were the same age as Paige.

"Give it back, Cody. Give it back or I'll—" The girl was pulling on a rag doll that the boy was holding ransom.

The neighbor woman ran out the front door. "Cody, give your sister her doll, and both of you, get back in this cottage!"

"Hi, Alice." My aunt waved from the screened porch. "Getting settled in I see."

Alice looked apologetically at my aunt. "We've been here one day and they're already at it," she said, defeated. "Twins. You're lucky to have yours so many years apart."

"It still doesn't make it easier. At least you got to get through the diapers all at the same time."

Paige walked over to them. "Hey, Callie, want to play?"

We slipped by my mom and my aunt who were still on the porch and went in the back door so they wouldn't see my dirty clothes. It led to a hallway where the bathroom was immediately on the right. It was so small that it only had a toilet in it, no sink. Straight ahead was the shower stall, separated only by a frosty white shower curtain.

We crept into our bedroom.

"I can't believe you swam out to Slippery Rock. That was brave," Wendy whispered. "I wouldn't have done it, even if I knew how to swim."

"I can't believe it either," I said, rubbing my muscles. "I really didn't think I was going to make it."

"Please don't tell my parents. I would get into so much trouble," Wendy said.

I ran my fingers across my mouth, turned an invisible key, and threw it away.

"I didn't know you smoked," I whispered.

"I don't," Wendy whispered back.

"I don't like it," I confessed.

"I don't think anybody does, but whatever Julie does, the rest do."

"Why does she act so stuck up?"

"Popularity. It changes people. When I was ten, I had to have my appendix out, and she was the only one from camp who came to the hospital to see me. She used to be real nice. Now she just pretends."

I fumbled in my suitcase for some dry clothes. I changed as fast as I could. I didn't have any brothers or sisters so I felt weird being naked in front of Wendy. I saw her looking at me and felt myself blush.

It was awkward and I think she felt it too because she quickly said, "I'll show you my scar." Standing in front of me, she raised her T-shirt and lowered her shorts a little to show me. It was still raised and angry looking.

"Did it hurt?"

"It did at first, but it doesn't anymore. It's just a reminder now."

After I changed clothes, we went to the living room and sat down next to Paige. The couch still smelled moldy from being closed up all winter.

My aunt and my mom were at the table sipping coffee. They talked in whispers and every so often, my aunt reached over to touch my mother's hand. I tried to listen but Wendy and Paige kept asking me questions.

Not long after, Uncle Butch's station wagon pulled up to the cottage. He came inside, went right to my mom, and hugged her. "It's so good to see you again. It's been too long." He threw the car keys and his Lucky Strike cigarette pack on the side table next to the chair.

"It has been too long," Mom said, hugging him back.

"Hi, Uncle Butch," I said.

"Well, hello," he said. He came over and hugged me. I missed my father and it felt good to be hugged by him. "You're all grown up. Pretty, too. You definitely get that from our side of the family, right, Jo?" He laughed.

"Yeah, right," Mom said. "Like Mama always said, 'We come from good stock.'"

"Girls, set the table for dinner please," my aunt said and disappeared into the kitchen.

A few minutes later, my aunt came in from the kitchen and placed bowls of fried chicken and mashed potatoes in front of us. Mom brought in sliced tomatoes and corn on the cob. My stomach grumbled when I saw all that good food. After my dad left, Mom didn't cook much. We usually just heated up frozen dinners and ate in front of the TV and watched *The Brady Bunch*. I always imagined my mom re-marrying and I would have a whole houseful of step sisters and we would all be happy, and I would never feel alone again because me and my new step sisters would all be best friends.

Uncle Butch sat down at the head of the table and ran his fingers through his dark hair, the same color as Mom's.

It was hard to believe that he and my mom had ever been my age. One time my mom showed me an old black-and-white photo of them when she was thirteen and he was twelve. Looking at the dog-eared photograph, I couldn't imagine my mother ever that pretty, with her long dark hair framing her face. She cut her hair short before I was born and always styled it up and away from her face. She seemed mysterious in the photo, like she was hiding something.

"Uncle Butch?" I asked.

"Yeah, sweetie?"

"What about Grandpa?" I knew a little about my grandmother, and even remembered her before she died, but I had never met my grandfather. Mom never talked about him much so I thought this was the perfect time to find out more about my relatives.

"Well . . ." He put down his fork as if trying to find the memories.

"Mom said he smoked a pipe." I was hoping this would jog a memory loose because Mom had hers all wrapped up tight in her memory cave.

"He did smoke a pipe. I still remember the sweet smell of cherry tobacco. I love that smell," Uncle Butch said.

"I hate that smell. It makes me sick to my stomach," Mom said.

"What? You used to love it," Uncle Butch said.

"Well, that's what got him in the end, isn't it. Throat cancer. Now I can't stand the smell. It reminds me of death. It destroyed his vocal cords and he couldn't even speak in the end. But his mind was sharp. It was a shame that he was trapped inside his own head and he couldn't tell us what he was thinking." She stopped abruptly. I knew she had more to say. I saw it in the urgency in her eyes.

I shifted in my seat, sorry I brought it up.

"He also loved hot sauce on just about everything, including eggs." Uncle Butch's voice was low, easing into the heated air like a light breeze. "Remember, Jo? There was always a bottle on the table and he used it like salt. We always had plenty of Frank's hot sauce because he worked at the factory."

My mom's face softened. "And he loved to listen to the Cincinnati Reds on his transistor radio. Everyone in the house had to be quiet when he was listening to his baseball game." As quickly as her face softened, it suddenly squeezed up into a tight ball of wrinkles. "He had a mean streak, too. Let's not forget that."

"Yeah, he did. But that's what made him unique."

"Unique? Is that what you call it?" Mom's voice pitched up as if her memory cave was shaking itself loose.

"He wasn't always like that."

"Really? Well, you remember him *your* way, and I'll remember him *my* way." Mom took a deep breath. "One time he got a parking ticket and do you know what he did?" She didn't wait for an answer. "He collected enough pennies to pay the fine and put them in a jar."

"He paid in pennies?" I was amused, but Mom wasn't. Her voice was strained.

"Not only that, he poured molasses in that jar and took it right to the police station. Told them it wasn't fair, and he shouldn't have gotten that ticket in the first place. He was parked in an emergency zone and he had an emergency when he got the ticket, so it shouldn't count."

"What was the emergency?" I asked.

"Well, as he explained to the police officer, he was parked in the emergency zone in front of the police station because he was inside paying for his first ticket and if that wasn't an emergency he didn't know what was."

"That wasn't mean, that was just funny," Uncle Butch said.

My mom cut him a look. "Yeah, that was hilarious. I laughed so hard I cried." She cocked her head, like she was remembering something. "Why did we always have so many pennies in the house? I never understood that."

"They grew up in the Great Depression. Every penny counted back then," Uncle Butch said.

"You're right, I guess."

"Do you remember taking pennies to the railroad track so we could flatten them?" Uncle Butch asked.

"That brings back memories. Do you still have them?"

"I do." Uncle Butch got up from the table and disappeared into the master bedroom. He came back and handed something to Mom.

"I can't believe it." She turned it over in her hand and examined it like it was a diamond. "Those were good times, huh Butch? We always had each other's back." She looked at the penny, and then she handed it to me. "Here. Penny for your thoughts."

I looked at the penny but it no longer resembled a coin. I couldn't make heads or tails of it. It was smooth and flat. And it wasn't a circle anymore, it was oval.

"Is it worth anything?" I asked.

"Well, I don't think you can buy penny candy with it," Mom said.

I rubbed my fingers over its smooth surface, and then tucked it into my pocket for safe keeping.

After dinner, I sat at the table with my cousins and played cards, but I couldn't concentrate. Mom was on the couch next to Aunt Lori and Uncle Butch sat in his chair that seemed to have taken on his shape. They talked quietly in that low voice they used when they didn't want "the youngsters" to hear, so I put away my Mickey Mouse ears and gave up trying to figure it out.

I thought about how I ended up here. About how my dad abandoned us and set off a whole chain of events that landed me so far from home. Mom drove all day and I co-piloted. During the drive, we sang, laughed, told stories. I never felt closer to her. But, now that I thought about her leaving tomorrow, there was no more laughter in my heart, and the summer was only beginning.

CHAPTER TWO
GOODBYE

THE NEXT MORNING after breakfast, it was time to say goodbye to Mom. My bruises reared up and punched harder against my stomach. I had a hard time keeping breakfast down.

We gathered by the car. Mom hugged Uncle Butch first. "Take care of her. She's the only thing I have left."

That was the first time I ever heard her say anything that might even remotely suggest that maybe Dad was never coming back to us. It scared me because her hope that he was coming back was the only thing keeping her going.

After she hugged everyone else she walked over to me.

"Bye, honey, have a good time." She kissed the top of my head. "And promise to call me every Saturday, okay?"

"I promise."

As she wrapped her arms around me, I couldn't help thinking about my dad, and how I never got to say goodbye to him. I couldn't hold back the huge wave of emotion that was storming inside of me. The pain squeezed up through my chest and it felt like I couldn't breathe. Tears streamed from my eyes. I wondered if she was ever going to come back for me or if this was our last goodbye, too.

I hugged her and whispered, "Please don't leave."

Her eyes filled with sadness, and, in that moment, she was someone other than my mother. "I have to, baby girl. I have to take care of some business back home."

"Then take me back with you. I can help."

"If there was any other way, I'd take it. Besides, I'm just a phone call away."

That was true, but not true at the same time. She was one phone call, two states, and eight hours away.

"Be brave."

I would do anything for my mom, so when she said that, I wiped away my tears and looked her right in the eye so she would understand. I *would* be brave for her. It was an unspoken promise. I smiled my sad smile at her and she smiled her sad smile back at me.

As she drove away, I watched until she blurred at the edges as if she was disappearing into another dimension. I sat quietly on the couch for a long time, trying not to throw up. Uncle Butch went to work as soon as my mom left and my aunt and cousins busied themselves, leaving me alone to sulk by myself. I rubbed the smooth surface of the penny Mom gave me, trying to hold on to the only thing I had left of her.

After a few hours, my aunt made lunch and insisted I eat something. I sat down next to Wendy at the kitchen table and poured a glass of milk. Then I forced a peanut butter and jelly sandwich down my throat, which was hard because it still felt like it was squeezed shut.

I sulked on the couch and when my aunt noticed she came over and sat down next to me. She put her arm on my shoulder. "It will all work out. Promise."

I disagreed. It didn't seem like anything was going to work out. I pulled my knees to my chest and wrapped my arms around them.

"Honey, I know you're sad, but you can't mope around all summer."

BUT I DID mope around. I moped around All Day, even though my cousins tried repeatedly to get me off of the couch and in a better mood. I started to understand the sadness that my mother just couldn't shake. I was beginning to wonder if I was going to end up just like her, and I was scared.

Uncle Butch came home, and I was forced to eat dinner and pretend to feel alive, but I just went through the motions to appear normal.

After dinner, I asked if I could take a shower.

"Sure, go ahead, but you better get used to quick showers. The water only stays warm for a couple of minutes," Aunt Lori said.

I went through the kitchen, which lead to a hallway where the shower and bathroom were. I walked into the shower stall and undressed. I reached my hand out to hang my clothes on the hook. The shower stall was so small that I could touch the sides with my hands outstretched and still have a bend in my elbows. I was thankful for the running water, although the stream was just a sputter. Raising my face to the showerhead, I let the water wash away the day's grime. The tepid water quickly gave way to cold, matching my mood.

I rubbed my eyes and reached for the towel. My fingers felt the bar where the towel should have been, but it was empty.

I stood dripping and cold, so I yelled out, "Um . . . can I get a towel please?"

"Here you go." Uncle Butch pushed a towel toward me. His silhouette behind the frosted white shower curtain looked like a bear lumbering before me.

"Your Aunt Lori wanted to make sure you had a clean, dry towel."

Blinking away soap, I reached out and grabbed it. "Thanks."

The rest of the night was quiet, and I couldn't see a thing when I went to the bathroom. When I got back into bed, I pulled the covers over my head to feel safe, just like when I was little. My heart ached for my mother and I cried softly into my pillow until I fell asleep.

CHAPTER THREE
CRAZY MARY

THE NEXT MORNING I lay in bed waiting for my cousins to wake up. They slept in the bunk beds across from me. The sun ripped through the curtains, creating broken shadows in the room.

It reminded me of the dream I had last night. I dreamt of running with the wind at my back. I swayed with the wind, dancing with the invisible breeze. Then it turned dark and the grass was no longer green but brown and dying. I felt its invisible strength as huge rushing shadows appeared across the field and began chasing me. I was running and running but I was staying in one place. I couldn't get away from the unseen thing chasing me.

I shuddered. Even though it was summer, I was cold. I wasn't usually cold. But it wasn't just the weather; it was the weather on top of everything else. On top of me being here.

I listened as my aunt drifted out of her bedroom and into the kitchen, where she started breakfast. A pan scraped against the burner and then I heard the clicking of the gas stove lighting. A few minutes later, the smell of bacon filled the cottage.

Aunt Lori served me breakfast while Uncle Butch was just finishing up. He was eating with his fingers, picking up his bacon and dipping it into the yolk of his egg with one hand while holding the newspaper with the other. He picked up his "World's Best Dad" mug and slurped his coffee, making the liquid gurgle between his lips.

"Are you going to work today, Daddy?" Paige asked. She was still small enough to climb into his lap and get a hug.

"It's not summer vacation for me, sweetie." He lowered the newspaper from his face and unfolded Paige from his lap. He rose from the table and kissed her on the top of her head.

After he left, Wendy flopped on the couch next to me. "What do you want to do now?"

"Let's watch TV."

Wendy laughed. "We don't have a TV here because we can't get any reception. We don't have any phone lines either."

My aunt came into the room with folded laundry in her hands.

"How am I supposed to call my mom every Saturday?" I asked, panicking.

"We have a phone at the house in Mount Adams, sweetie. I'll make sure you can call your mom on Saturdays," Aunt Lori said.

I felt a little better but there was still nothing to do. Wendy sensed my boredom.

"Let's go to the playground," Wendy said.

"Wendy, take your sister with you."

"Oh, Mom."

"You hardly have to watch her. Just let her tag along."

I didn't mind her hanging around, but it sure did bother Wendy.

We walked to the playground with Paige straggling behind us.

"Wait up, guys, wait for me," Paige said, trying to catch up.

Wendy snickered and started walking faster.

"No fair! I can't walk that fast," Paige said.

Wendy giggled, continuing her sprint to the playground.

When we got there, Paige went to the sand box while we took charge of the swings.

Next to the swings was a large pool surrounded by a chain link fence and next to that were two tennis courts, also fenced in. A large grassy field separated the two. We could see the pavilion on the other side of the field. A lawnmower roared in the distance and I smelled fresh cut grass. I loved that smell. It reminded me of home, of my dad cutting our own grass. After he was done, I would help him rake up the clippings and put them into bags. The smell made me realize how much I missed him. How much I missed my mom, too.

"Hey, look, it's New Girl and Wendy." Julie walked to the side of the swings and stopped just short of me hitting her upside her face with my feet, startling me.

"Hey, Julie. What's up?" I said.

"Going to the river. Want to come?"

"No, can't. Got to watch my sister," Wendy said.

"Where's your entourage?" I asked with more sarcasm than I intended.

"New Girl, you're trying to be cool, but it's not working. My entourage is already at the river, waiting for me. So, do you want to come or not?"

"We have to watch Paige."

"No, *she* has to watch Paige. You could come to the river with me if you wanted." Julie crossed her arms over her chest and stared at me.

I thought about it. About when Julie looked at me after my swim, it made me feel excited and scared at the same time. But I couldn't leave Wendy and Paige behind. I'm sure she put me in this tight spot on purpose. "Well, if Wendy has to watch Paige, then I have to watch Paige too. I'm her company."

"No you don't, New Girl. Wendy has it covered, don't you Wendy?"

"Well, yeah," Wendy said.

Julie moved closer to me. I could smell her citrus shampoo as her hair fell forward around her face. "See, Wendy has it covered, so get off the swing and follow me to the river."

"No," I said louder than I intended.

Julie looked at me wide-eyed. I could tell this was not a word she heard often. "What?"

When she looked at me she made me want to sing and yell at the same time. I was conflicted. Wendy looked at me with the biggest smile so I knew what I had to do. I had to stick up for Wendy, so I corralled all my courage. "Well, it's like this. Blood is thicker than water and I want to stay here with my cousins."

"Okay, suit yourself. But you don't know what you're missing." She turned on her heels and was off toward the river, her long hair glowing in the sun.

"What was that about?" Wendy asked.

"That was another challenge I think."

"Did you pass?" Wendy asked.

"I don't think so. I think I just made her mad."

"Well, thanks for staying with us," Wendy said, swaying on the swing with her feet on the ground.

"No problem. Like I said, blood is thicker than water."

"Come on, I'll show you a haunted house," Wendy said.

Paige jumped out of the sandbox and ran up to us. "Wait up, guys, wait for me. I want to come."

We followed the road to the entrance of the camp, passing through tall pine trees. Paige tried to keep up but mostly fumbled behind.

On the edge of the neighborhood, an old house stood tall on a hill, an aging queen overlooking her domain.

As we reached the house, Wendy pointed and whispered, "That's Crazy Mary's place."

We were standing on the dirt road in front the house just yards away, scared to go near it.

I was sure the house had a view of the river and the entire camp from the third story window. It reminded me of a haunted house in a horror movie. All that was missing was the spooky music. The white paint was peeling and the steps led to a decaying wrap-around porch. In front of the porch were wild bushes laced with spider webs. In the front yard was a huge weeping willow with its branches touching the ground. Cement containers made for flowers were overflowing with weeds. The screen door was cracked open, squeaking when the wind blew it back and forth. Black shutters were on either side of the windows, some a little off kilter. Cats sunned themselves around the house and bowls of cat food and water littered the porch.

"She's the only one who lives here year round anymore and owns all that land over there." Wendy pointed to an open field.

Tall grass danced in the breeze. It seemed to me that the grass could be the hair on a giant's head peeking up from below the earth.

"I heard she killed her husband and inherited this place. No one ever sees her and there's a rumor that she only comes out at night."

Mystery hung in the air.

"There are so many cats," I said.

"Keep your eyes open for Crazy Mary," Wendy warned.

"Why?" I kept my attention on the cats.

"She hates kids, and she doesn't like visitors, either."

I walked to the steps and reached out to pet an orange cat. Wendy stayed on the road, watching me closely, while Paige followed me. "Well, we're not visiting her; we're visiting the cats, right, Paige?"

"Yep," Paige said.

"That's just a technicality," Wendy said. "I'm not visiting the cats, *you guys* are. I don't want to have anything to do with it, especially with Crazy Mary."

"What's her story anyway? Do you think she really killed her husband?"

"I don't know. That's what people say. Why else would she be such a loner?"

"She can't be all bad, if she's feeding all these cats," I said. "I don't trust people who don't like animals. You can tell a lot about people by the way they treat animals."

"I didn't say she murdered her *cats*."

A cat brushed up against my leg and I jumped. I could tell it was a kitten as a tiny flash of black disappeared under the porch. A minute later another cat jumped up on the railing of the porch and meowed at us.

"Look at that pretty black-and-white one," I said. I walked slowly up the steps toward it. As soon as I got close enough to touch it, the cat jumped back down and disappeared under the porch.

"Looks like it doesn't like you," Wendy said.

"Here kitty, kitty." I looked as hard as I could under the porch, but it was too dark and all I could see were two pairs of gleaming eyes. A tiny meow came from deep beneath the house.

"Here kitty, kitty," Paige said, following me around.

"Come on. Let's go," Wendy said nervously.

"It's okay. I want to see the cats."

"That's not a good idea."

"I'm just going to . . ." I heard a ping against a window, scaring me silly, and we ran back to where Wendy was standing on the dirt road in front of the house. Then we heard another ping and looked at each other in disbelief.

"What was that?" I asked.

"I don't know. We'd better get back, though," Wendy said.

I looked in the direction of the noise. My eyes widened when an older woman peeked from behind the curtain of an upstairs window, then disappeared quickly.

"I saw her!" I said, tugging on Wendy's sleeve.

"What?" Wendy asked.

"She was right there in the window," I said, pointing up to the second story.

We heard a girl laugh. We turned around and saw Julie hiding behind the weeping willow tree with a handful of little rocks. She stepped out from the tree.

"Scared you, didn't I? You should have seen your faces," she said, laughing at us.

"That wasn't funny, Julie," I said, turning to leave.

"Not so brave today, are you, New Girl?"

I walked to the end of the dirt road and could barely make out the name on the weathered mailbox. It read, "Weaver."

That night in bed, I reviewed everything in my head and the three things that kept coming back to me were—the woman behind the curtain, Julie, and my mother.

I wondered about the woman behind the curtain and what secrets, what horrors kept her locked inside her house.

I thought about Julie and how much I wanted to be like her.

And, I thought about my mother. I finally realized how *alone* she must feel, because now I was in the same boat.

CHAPTER FOUR
ELEPHANT IN THE ROOM

ON FRIDAY NIGHT, we had big doings—a dance at the camp's pavilion. It was the first dance of the summer and a time of excitement. Wendy put on a yellow sundress and encouraged me to wear one, too, but I told her I hadn't worn a dress in years and wasn't about to start now. Instead, I wore blue plaid shorts and a white cotton shirt. Paige wore a matching short set with sunflowers on it, which brought out her brown eyes and hair.

I looked at Wendy, all dressed up for the occasion. "Well, you think you're all that, and a piece of pie."

"Shut up," she said, hitting my shoulder.

When we were ready, we gathered on the porch.

"Well, don't you girls look pretty," Uncle Butch said. I was beginning to feel like I was part of a family again.

We walked to the pavilion together, which was across the big grassy field at the edge of the camp where the cottages ended. Inside, picnic tables lined the edges of the pavilion. In the center was a dance floor and against the back wall was a band. On the far left was a small concession stand. Huge white ceiling fans hung overhead, cooling us from the heat.

People trickled in from all directions, young and old alike. We chose the table closest to the door and sat down while my aunt and uncle stood at the edge of the table greeting people as they entered. I looked around for Julie and the gang, but didn't see them.

Uncle Butch put down a bottle wrapped in a brown paper bag and some plastic red cups. Then he threw down a pack of Lucky Strike cigarettes.

"Alice, Bob! Over here," he called, motioning the couple over. They also had a brown bag and plastic cups.

I recognized the woman as the mother of the twins, Cody and Callie. She had long blond hair parted in the middle and wore a flowered sundress that ended above her knees.

"They're no doubt trying to get in as much practice as possible to win the dance contest this year," Uncle Butch muttered to Aunt Lori, covering his mouth with the back of his hand as he spoke.

"Don't be an old fart," Aunt Lori said, hitting him lightly on the shoulder.

"I see Dr. Ferguson made it with his new wife. She's probably thinking that she done hit the jack pot marrying him. How many does that make now, three?" Uncle Butch asked.

"You're incorrigible," Aunt Lori said.

Dr. Ferguson was older and wore a beige suit with a straw hat that covered his thinning grey hair. He had round spectacles and a chubby face. He also had a grey mustache and a round belly, with the chain of a pocket watch stretched across his front. He pulled out a silver flask and took a long pull from it, then offered it to the young lady by his side. She shook her head and locked an elbow around his.

Before long, the pavilion was full and the wooden floor squeaked under the weight. We sat across from Cody and Callie. They looked like six-year-old angels sitting across from us with their blond curls outlining their faces. The light shined through their hair, creating halos around their heads.

"Paige likes Cody," Wendy whispered above the noise.

"Do not."

"Do too."

I looked around for the gang again, worried they wouldn't show. The crowd blocked my view but after a few minutes, I finally saw them on the other side of the pavilion in the back. They stood by the picnic table next to the exit. I waved and Reds waved back. This was the first time I had seen him without his Reds baseball cap. He was cute.

"Wendy, go to the snack bar and get us a bottle of pop and a bucket of ice," Uncle Butch said, handing her a ten.

"Hey," Reds said as he approached us. "Come over to our table. We got some . . ." He put his thumb to his lip and tilted his head back.

Wendy seemed to understand immediately what he was implying, but I was puzzled.

"Alcohol," she whispered in my ear.

"Oh," I said.

"We'll be right over, as soon as I get this back to my dad," Wendy said.

"Get us some pop and ice, too, and bring it over when you come," Reds said, disappearing into the crowd.

Wendy set the Coke and ice on the table while Aunt Lori and Uncle Butch were busy talking. We hightailed it back toward the snack bar, eager to meet up with the gang. Paige, who was talking to Cody and Callie, didn't notice us leave.

The singer blew into the microphone and the excitement grew. A loud popping noise echoed from the speakers. "Let's get this party started."

Hands clapped, feet stomped, and the dance floor came alive with the first song as we ordered from the pimply kid behind the concession counter. A black-haired girl behind the counter looked at me curiously. I turned to the dance floor and saw Aunt Lori and Uncle Butch dancing, the crowd shifting to the sides to give them room.

"Hey, look," I said, nudging Wendy's shirt sleeve.

"Yep, there they go," Wendy said.

"What dance is that?" I asked.

"It's called the jitterbug. They'll be at it all night."

I hung onto every movement as they danced in the center of the floor. They moved so closely to the beat of the music that they *became* the music. I wondered if I would ever be able to dance like that. They became a single unit of grace. Other couples danced together, but Aunt Lori and Uncle Butch stole the show with their fancy footwork and elaborate turns.

"How do two people dance like that without talking, without knowing what the other is going to do?" I asked, impressed.

"They've been dancing together like that a long time," Wendy said, unimpressed.

After we ordered the Coke and ice, we weaved our way over to the gang. Julie was standing at the head of the table with Tommy. Freckles leaned against the picnic table, a camouflage backpack next to his feet.

"Well, well, look who it is, New Girl and Wendy," Julie said.

Reds walked up from behind. "Leave them alone, Julie. They brought the pop and ice."

I liked Reds. He was always sticking up for us.

Wendy placed the Coke and ice in front of Julie. She was the tootsie roll center in a lollipop crowd. Everyone circled around her, wanting to be by her side. She had a way about her that seemed magical. You know, the one that had *it*, whatever that was. You knew it when you spotted it, or were in the presence of it, but it was too difficult to explain.

She was wearing a mini skirt and a tight shirt. She looked like a cheerleader. All that was missing were the pom-poms. *Rah, rah, ree, kick 'em in the knee. Rah, rah, rass . . . kick 'em in the other knee.* She had red-painted fingernails with matching toenails. She looked so grown up. And well, I didn't. I should have re-thought the dressing up thing.

"Put ice in the cups," Julie said to me.

I filled each cup with ice, handed them to Julie, who filled them with Coke and handed them to Freckles, who then added what looked like whiskey. It was a sophisticated assembly line and I felt important. I was deliriously happy to be in her circle. The pounding of the drum echoed in my heart, beating forcefully against my chest. It was loud and magical. Other kids looked at me with jealous eyes as I huddled around the queen.

Freckles handed a cup to each of us.

I took mine hesitantly. "Thanks," I said meekly and glanced over to see if Aunt Lori and Uncle Butch were watching. They were too busy dancing to notice anything we were doing. Julie took a sip, then looked at me.

"Well, New Girl, you going to look at it or drink it?" Julie asked.

I put the cup to my lips and swallowed as everyone watched. It burned my throat all the way to my stomach and left me breathless. I faked a smile and nodded my head. "That's good."

First smoking, now drinking. I was surely going to hell for this, and I hoped it was worth it. I was breaking all my mom's rules in the first week.

With music pulsing in my ears, I swayed back and forth with the beat. Julie leaned close to Tommy and whispered in his ear. Flirting came easy to her and she practiced it often. She swiped the loose hair from her forehead. I turned into her hair, trying to listen through the corn silk strands draped close to her face, but I still couldn't hear her.

After their drinks were finished, Julie and Tommy moved onto the dance floor. Their hips moved to the beat as they moved back and forth rhythmically. They looked good dancing together because they were both tall. Tommy held up his hand and Julie turned under his arm, flipping her hair across his face as she did.

Next, Owl and Wendy paired up. Owl looked a little reluctant, but before the song was halfway through, they were dancing sloppily next to Julie and Tommy. I took a gulp from my drink and my stomach fluttered as Reds approached me from the other side of the table.

"Come on, let's dance," he said. He held out his sweaty hand.

"I don't know how . . ." I started, but he took my hand and pulled me gently onto the dance floor. My heart started beating faster.

Julie saw me, gave me the thumbs-up sign, and smiled. Reds and I were surrounded by the dancing crowd and I was trying to keep up, but mostly we stumbled around each other.

When he raised his hand for me to turn right, I turned left and lost my balance. I tried to find my place and grow light on my feet, but it was no use. His hands sweated in mine and he wasn't bending at the knees.

I was feeling the heat in my cheeks, either from embarrassment or the whiskey, I didn't know which. We were struggling. Flame-faced, we finally gave up and went back to our picnic table where Freckles was waiting.

I really noticed Reds then. He had black hair in a thick crop of curls. His eyes were emerald green. He smiled, revealing even white teeth. I forgot my shyness and smiled back. My head felt light as I got caught up in the excitement of the evening. It felt good. I released some of the anxiety I had been carrying around all week worrying about my mom.

Reds put his hand on my shoulder, guiding me through the crowd toward the exit in the back. Outside, he held my hand while we left the dancing to everyone else. The music wasn't as loud, but I still had a hard time hearing him.

"Want a cigarette?" Reds asked.

"What?"

"Cigarette?" he asked, handing the pack to me.

"No." I felt awkward. I no sooner got the word out before he leaned over and kissed me on the lips. He smelled like cigarettes and tasted like whiskey. I didn't like it.

The screen door slammed and I looked in that direction, glad for the interruption.

"There you are," Julie said as she came over and draped her arm sloppily around my shoulder. I could smell her hair. It smelled as if lemons and oranges danced together creating the perfect citrusy aroma.

When we got back inside, I watched my aunt and uncle dance some more. Paige and Cody had locked elbows and were twirling in the middle of the dance floor. Callie was twirling by herself next to them.

At eight o'clock, the singer spoke into the microphone. "Okay, kids, anyone who's not eighteen or older, it's time for you to leave." When we didn't shuffle out fast enough, he repeated, "All those younger than eighteen, we have to say good night."

Julie whispered something into Wendy's ear as Uncle Butch waved us over from across the dance floor. Wendy grabbed my arm and I waved bye to everyone. I followed Wendy through the dispersing crowd. Parents huddled their children outside, giving last instructions. Alice was talking to a girl who looked like she was a couple of years older than us. I guessed she was Cody and Callie's babysitter. It seemed all the kids were outside now, being shooed away.

Uncle Butch followed us outside the pavilion to give us our instructions while Aunt Lori stayed inside. "Get Paige to bed and you can stay up another hour, but you can't leave the cottage." Uncle Butch swayed while he was speaking. A warm breeze enveloped me. As we started to leave, I heard Uncle Butch's voice.

"Hey, Alice. Have you ever seen my imitation of an elephant?"

I turned around to see what was happening. He was standing with both pockets turned inside out of his pants. Then he pretended to unzip his fly. "Get it?"

"You're incorrigible," Alice said, waving him away with a swoosh of her hand.

That was the second time I heard that word in one night. Obviously, Uncle Butch was a pretty good example of it.

He raised both hands toward the sky. "Oh, come on, it's funny . . ."

Wendy grabbed my hand and we double-timed it back to the cottage, Paige running behind us to catch up. We put Paige to bed and waited for her to fall asleep. Fifteen long minutes passed before she fluttered into dreamland.

"Okay, here's the deal," Wendy whispered. "We're meeting the gang in the game room over there." She pointed out the window to our next destination. It was a cinder block building just off to the left of Uncle Butch's cottage.

"What if Paige wakes up, or your parents come back?"

"Don't worry." She hiccupped. "We can see the cottage from there, so if that happens, we'll just sneak in through the back door."

We entered the game room, and everyone was already there. The room had two pinball machines against the far wall and a pool table was in the center of the room. Julie and Tommy were holding hands, leaning against it.

Freckles finished pouring the last of the whiskey into our cups and held up the empty bottle. "Let's play spin the bottle."

We sat in a circle, boy—girl fashion. Everything seemed to be happening in slow motion. My head felt light, like I could fly away. I felt the heat in my cheeks and the tips of my ears. I couldn't stop smiling, even though nothing was really all that funny. My heart raced, but the whiskey stilled my inhibitions until I could no longer think of a good reason not to play.

The first to spin was Freckles. The bottle clanked on the concrete floor, spinning until the bottle finally rested on Julie. She got up and walked over to Freckles, who stood up too. He leaned in and pushed his lips firmly on hers. She broke away from the kiss first and then smirked at me as she sat back down.

Next, it was her turn to spin the bottle. With a great whoosh, it clanked around the circle, spinning, spinning. Finally it slowed and landed on me. Everyone looked at me.

"Now what?" I asked.

Julie walked over to me and sat down. "You've never played this before, have you?"

I shook my head. My heart fluttered as she leaned closer to me as if trying to connect to my lips. I shivered and turned my head quickly, causing her to kiss my cheek instead. Her breath was warm against my cheek.

"Well, New Girl. If it lands on someone of the same sex, you're supposed to kiss the person to the right." Leaning over, she kissed Reds directly on his lips. She held the back of his head and brought her open mouth to his. She didn't close her eyes like she had with Freckles. Instead she kept them focused on me. She pulled his head away from her after an intense minute of kissing and then smiled. My stomach fluttered.

After a few turns, Tommy gave the bottle a great spin and it landed on Wendy. He walked over to her slowly and closed his eyes, pressing his lips gently against hers. Julie harrumphed and ended the game then. Spinning the bottle was more than just a game; it was a measure of friendship. It seemed Wendy was crossing over Julie's measuring tape by kissing Tommy.

At the pavilion the music stopped. We heard a man's voice from across the pavilion. It was getting closer. "Come on, don't leave yet. The night is young."

Someone laughed a happy, genuine laugh. Even from a distance, I could tell it was Aunt Lori.

"Your parents are coming!" I squealed and grabbed Wendy's arm. We ran out the door and to the cottage with battery-powered feet without saying goodbye.

We turned off the light and jumped into our beds. A few minutes later, I heard the muffled voice of Uncle Butch as they entered the bedroom. "I can do it, Lori."

We both giggled, and I tucked deeper into my blanket, covering most of my face. I heard a drawer open.

"Butch, careful or you're going to bang your . . ."

"Ouch."

The bed squeaked against the wall next to me, followed by the slide of dresser drawers and then all was quiet, for a while.

Later, as my eyes closed, Uncle Butch spoke. I swear it was as if he were right next to me. "Come here, baby, and give me a little love."

My eyes blinked open. With my heart racing, I turned to look at Wendy on the bottom bunk. A slice of moonlight showed that her eyes were closed and by the heavy breathing, I guessed she was asleep.

"You're drunk," Aunt Lori said, shutting the bedroom door between us.

"Oh, come on, you said that last time." Uncle Butch's deep voice was muffled as if it was underwater.

I shoved my pillow over my head. I wished I were somewhere else—anywhere else. I heard the undeniable sound of a slap, and felt the sting on my own face as if it had happened to me.

"Don't, you're hurting me." Underwater voices again. "No." Another slap. "You're just like your father," Aunt Lori whimpered. "A mean nasty drunk who thinks he owns women. The apple doesn't fall far from the tree."

I pulled the afghan my grandmother had made over me and buried my face, trying to drown out the voices. A few minutes passed before I felt the bed bumping against the wall next to me. Repeatedly it bumped like the beating of a heart. The pounding became overwhelming. I thought of my favorite writer, Edgar Allan Poe. I was listening to my very own *Tell-Tale Heart*. I pushed the bed away using my feet so I wouldn't have to be near that wall with the beating heart inside it.

I was embarrassed. And confused. It changed the way I thought about sex. I thought it was something that was special between two people in love. Something private and magical that they shared with one another. But what I just heard was a drunk taking advantage of someone. Someone he was supposed to love and protect.

I wondered how Aunt Lori could put up with him. As far as I could see, she acted like every time he farted it was glorious. There was no glory to bad gas. Or bad people.

CHAPTER FIVE
DISCONNECTED

SATURDAY MORNING THE sun crept under my eyelids, forcing them open before I was ready. A dull headache made me groan. I knew Aunt Lori was already up because the radio was on. She always turned the radio on first thing in the morning. At my house, we never listened to the radio unless we were in the car.

"Good grief," I said, waking Wendy. She looked as sick as I felt.

The smell of bacon and eggs made my stomach turn, but I got out of bed and faked a smile at the breakfast table. Uncle Butch was absent, but it didn't seem to bother anyone, especially me after what I heard last night.

As we ate, small sounds came from Uncle Butch's bedroom. A groan, the slide of a dresser drawer, and his slippers sliding across the wooden floor. I looked at Wendy with apprehension.

"I have a Herculean headache," he said as he stepped into the room. His voice was gruff, like two bricks scraping together. He was wrapped in a bathrobe and his hair was all disheveled. "Where's the aspirin?"

Aunt Lori pushed him aside, avoiding eye contact with him. "I'll get it. Go sit down before your breakfast gets cold." When they danced, they were a single unit of grace. Now they were two people on opposite sides of the river.

She was singing to that song about rocking the boat. Singing the words as if she was trying to convince herself of their meaning. Singing her song of denial.

As he sat down at the table, Aunt Lori put the aspirin bottle in front of him abruptly. He pushed his plate away and struggled to open the lid. The aspirin rattled as he popped open the bottle. Dusty white tablets spilled on the floor. They sounded like a string of beads breaking.

"Dammit," he grumbled. He plucked three aspirin off the floor with his large fingers and shoved them into his mouth. He chewed a little before forcing them down his throat without water.

"Paige, pick the rest of those up for Daddy, would you, sweetie?" He drank coffee from his "World's Best Dad" cup.

She slid out of her chair and started picking up the pills and putting them back into the bottle. He narrowed his eyes at me. I wondered if he was trying to figure out if I heard anything last night. He seemed dark like my mother had at times and I didn't want any part of it.

Paige was being unusually quiet. Maybe she knew about my attempt to hide my headache. I wondered if my cousins had heard anything last night. I hoped they didn't, but I couldn't be sure. I felt bad for them.

Aunt Lori was a good cook, but my stomach was on a roller-coaster ride without me. I pushed the eggs around my plate, slid the bacon into my napkin, and tucked it into my pocket. The cats would appreciate it more than me today.

"Do you want to go see the cats with us?" I asked Paige.

"Yeah," Paige said, scooping her breakfast into her napkin.

Wendy evidently was not feeling well enough to object, so after breakfast we all walked to Crazy Mary's house, glad to get out of the cottage.

"How do you feel?" I asked Wendy as we crunched along the gravel road, passing the game room.

"Ugh, terrible."

"Me too, but it was so much fun," I said, pushing the tell-tale heart incident out of my mind.

"I'm glad Julie is talking to me again." She said it like it was an unspoken thank you, and I admit, it was nice having that sisterly bond between us.

"Yeah, me too."

We walked a little in silence. I thought about Aunt Lori and Uncle Butch, and how close they were last night dancing. How happy they seemed. Until . . . I pushed the thought out of my head.

"I want to learn how to dance before next week," I said. "I can't go slow dancing through life. I need to learn how to dance like your parents."

"You want to learn how to dance so you can dance with Reds, huh?" Wendy teased.

"Do not. Shut up."

Wendy turned dramatically, mouth open, and put her hand on my shoulder as if remembering an iron had been left on a hundred miles away from home. "How about that kiss last night?"

I knew she was talking about my kiss with Reds, but I turned the question around on her. "I know. Is Tommy a good kisser?"

"You kissed Tommy?" Paige asked.

"Shut up, and don't tell Mom or Dad," Wendy said, big-sistering her.

"I wasn't talking about the kiss with Tommy, I was talking about your kiss with Reds. I saw him kiss you outside last night," Wendy said.

"Oh, that." I tried to pretend that I wasn't excited, but that never worked for me.

"Yeah, that."

I smiled. "It was good, I guess."

Paige giggled and put her hand over her mouth.

"Don't tell, big mouth, or else . . ."

"Okay." Then Paige kicked her foot at the dirt. "Dad was drunk again last night, wasn't he?" She stuffed her hands into the pockets of her shorts, looking down.

"Yeah, Dad was drunk again." Wendy put her arm around Paige's shoulder. That was the first time I had seen her do that. Wendy always treated Paige like she was a pesky little sister. "Why?"

He acts weird when he's drinking," Paige said.

"Yeah, I know. Mom said he was born with it."

"With what?" I asked.

"The drinking disease. It runs in our family."

"What? That's not true," I said.

"Is so, Mom said. Said he was born with the drinking disease just like Grandpa."

Why didn't I know this stuff about my blood relatives?

"Did Grandpa drink too?" I asked.

"Every night. But he hid it from Grandma after she threatened to leave him if he didn't stop taking up with the devil. Craziness runs in the family too," Wendy said.

"What? You're kidding me."

"No, I'm not kidding," Wendy said. "Great Aunt Pat goes through queer spells every so often and no one can get through to her. Mom says she's just taking time off to find her brain."

I shook my head in disbelief. Is this what I had to look forward to? Bad blood running in the family? Would I end up like my mother with shadows crawling over me even at night? Or, would I become a drunk like Uncle Butch and Grandfather? I didn't want to go climbing up my family tree with all those rotten, broken branches. It seemed like my family was full of disease and sickness and I didn't want to become like any of them, not even my dad. I wanted more. I wanted to write in purple ink again.

We walked the rest of the way in silence until we got to Crazy Mary's house.

Paige's eyes lit up. "I'm scared."

I looked up at the window, but I didn't see the woman behind the curtain. "There's nothing to be afraid of, Paige. It's just a house, and we're here to see the cats anyway."

I walked slowly over to the steps while Paige and Wendy waited beside the road. I took the napkin out of my pocket and unwrapped the bacon from it. I held the bacon out for the cats to smell. "Here, kitty, kitty."

The black-and-white cat peeked out tentatively, sniffing the bacon. For a couple of minutes, I sat still as a statue so she would learn to trust me. Finally, she crept toward me, took the bacon, and ran back into the shadows. I noticed a movement next to the cat and held out another piece of bacon. Again, still as a statue, I waited. But this time I was rewarded by the appearance of a little black kitten, a spitting image of its mother. The kitten crept up slowly, its whiskers tickling my fingers.

"Wow," I whispered so I wouldn't scare it.

Paige came over to the steps to look, but Wendy stayed on the road in front of the house.

"It's a kitten!" she said.

"Quiet, Paige," I whispered. "Don't scare him."

Paige took a pinch of egg from her stash and held it out.

"He looks like an Oreo cookie with a little bit of cream on his chest," I said.

Unaware of us, the kitten ate the egg and smelled around for more. Slowly, he came out from the shadows. He wasn't as shy as his mother, but when we ran out of food, he quickly returned to his place next to her.

"I'm going to name him Oreo," I said.

I looked up at the front door and saw Crazy Mary peeking out from behind the curtain. She didn't appear mad, or weird, or crazy. Just curious. She looked at me with apprehensive eyes. Her white hair was pulled back into a neat bun making her look like an eloquent queen, all prim and proper. She was wearing a blue dress and she looked so—*normal.* I was expecting wild, wispy hair and big bulging eyes with spinning pupils.

I waved to her, trying to be friendly.

She smiled at me, then stepped out of view.

"What are you doing?" Wendy said. "She's crazy! And she hates kids."

"Sorry, but she doesn't seem as crazy as everyone says she is. Plus she smiled at me, so she couldn't hate kids that much.

I think she just needs someone to care about her. Maybe she's lonely. I would be, if I was locked up in a big house all day with no one to talk to."

"Me too," Paige said.

I smiled at her. For being so young, she seemed to have a lot of compassion, unlike Wendy.

"Let's go," Wendy said.

I looked at the door one last time before we left.

LATER, AT THE cottage, we played music on the radio and danced with each other. Wendy lifted her hand and I turned under it. Then she put both arms up and we both turned. We laughed.

"I want a turn!" Paige said.

Uncle Butch came on to the porch. "What are you girls up to?"

"We're trying to dance, Daddy," Paige said.

"We don't know how to dance like you and Mom, but it's still fun," Wendy said.

"Here, let me show you. Your mom can help too." He put his cigarette in the ash tray. "Lori, come here for a minute. We need your help. The girls want to learn how to dance."

"Is that so?" Aunt Lori came in from the kitchen, slinging a dish towel over her shoulder and wiping the strands of hair away from her face with the back of her hand.

"Daddy, are you really going to teach us how to dance?" Paige jumped up and down like a bean on a hot plate.

"Sure, honey."

"Chris wants to learn how to dance so she can dance with Dave," Paige said innocently.

I cringed, embarrassed. What a tattle-tale. "No I don't."

Wendy elbowed Paige. "Shut up."

"Does she?" Uncle Butch asked. He studied me, like I was some kind of secret he was trying to figure out, some sort of combination for him to unlock.

I sat on the arm of the couch embarrassed that Uncle Butch knew I liked Reds.

"Well then, let's get started," Uncle Butch said.

Aunt Lori held out her hands and asked me to join her. Then Paige and Wendy stood in front of each other joining hands as my uncle told us what to do.

"Now, when I say, lift your arms for a turn. Chris and Wendy, you will be the men, or leaders, so you will hold up your left arm to let the ladies turn under them."

"What do you mean?" I asked. "Do the men always lead? Why can't the ladies ever lead?"

"Because. It's the rule. The men are always the leaders," Aunt Lori said.

"That's right. Every man should know how to lead and every woman should learn how to follow, right, honey?"

"That's right, sweetie," Aunt Lori agreed.

Wendy and I held up our left hands and Paige and Aunt Lori turned underneath them, Aunt Lori ducking to clear my raised hand.

Paige squealed, "I'm a lady!"

Next we worked on footwork. Step tap, step tap, rock step. This was a bit more complicated but after practicing a while, we got the hang of it.

Uncle Butch kept directing us. "When you raise your hand, make a bridge for the lady to turn under it, and then use your other hand to guide her through the turn."

We got lost in the music and soon, we were actually dancing with each other. I was having fun.

"Let's change partners," Uncle Butch said.

I hesitated, but Uncle Butch grabbed my hand and Aunt Lori took Wendy's. Paige directed our turns.

Uncle Butch danced with experience. He lifted his arm and his other hand on my back gently guided me through the turn. Then he showed off some fancy footwork. I was following his lead and knew what he wanted me to do through various hand signals. It was like a secret sign language.

I got carried away, spinning and laughing. It was so much fun, and I turned again, but my uncle's hand never left my body, and his fingers brushed against my breasts as I spun. I pulled my hand away from his and stopped dancing. I looked around to see if anyone noticed, but they weren't looking in my direction. His hands always seemed to be reaching for me and touching me in some way or another, like he was trying to figure out whether I was real or not.

"Okay, that's enough dancing for one day," Uncle Butch said.

"That was fun," Paige said.

"Now what?" Wendy asked.

Uncle Butch walked over to the table and picked up the car keys.

"I'm going to drive Chris over to the house so she can call her mom."

"I want to come," Wendy said.

"I think I'll just take Chris myself so she can talk to her mom in private. She doesn't need you around bothering her when she's on the phone. Besides, you guys have been glued to each other all week. Give her some breathing space."

I hadn't been apart from Wendy since the moment I arrived, except for showers and bathroom breaks. I actually liked having her around. She was a sister I never had. "She won't bother me, really."

"Let her go, she won't get in the way. Plus, I need you to go to the grocery store, and she can help," Aunt Lori said, handing him a grocery list that had been tucked into her apron pocket.

He hesitated. "Let's go, then. I want to get back before dark."

We followed him out the door to the station wagon.

Wendy sat up front while I sat in the back. The ride was quiet. I had noticed during the week that Uncle Butch didn't talk much. He turned on the radio, which was playing oldies. I didn't know most of the songs, so I busied myself by looking out the window. The sun was setting, turning the sky pink, and the clouds looked like they were made of cotton candy.

He kept checking his rearview mirror every couple of minutes, looking at me. Smiling at me like he was watching a private movie and I was the movie star. All that was missing was the buttery popcorn in his lap. I got a major creep vibe from him. I'm glad Wendy came along.

Blowing the horn, Uncle Butch yelled at the car in front of him. "Get out of the way, you old bag!" He swerved the car into the next lane, passed the Cadillac, and almost cut the driver off as he swerved in front of her, muttering under his breath. The only thing I could make out was, "Too old to be driving, hag," and a lot more words like that.

After fifteen minutes he turned down a one-way street. He navigated to avoid the pot holes, taking the curves just right. I could tell he travelled this road many times before.

"We're here." He turned off the motor and it kicked over once and died.

We walked up the steps and entered the kitchen from the side door. The house was dark and smelled of rotten onions. I heard the click of a light switch and gradually everything came into focus. The onions were on the counter in a pool of goo.

"It stinks in here!" Uncle Butch carefully picked up the mesh bag and threw it in the trash. He lifted up the phone mounted on the wall and dialed the number that would connect me to my mother. I would have looked around more, but the rotten onion smell was burning my eyes. Wendy went into the other room and turned on the television. Uncle Butch disappeared upstairs to where the bedrooms were.

I counted the rings. I knew how sad and alone she was. I thought of the day she left me here and I felt tears welling up behind my eyelids.

After five rings, she finally answered the phone. "Hello?"

I took a deep breath of air. I felt like I had just burst through the surface after being underwater for too long. "Mom?"

"Chris, is that you, honey?"

"Yeah, it's me. What took you so long to answer? Is everything okay?"

"Everything's fine. I was in the other room, lying down. I didn't hear the phone at first, that's all." She sighed as if collecting her thoughts.

I had a whole list of things to tell her about, but all of her sadness seemed to be vibrating through the phone line, so I said the thing I was thinking the most. "I miss you."

"I miss you too. Are you having a good time?"

How was I going to tell her that I was having the time of my life like she said I would? "Yeah, Mom. I'm having fun. Every morning we go down to the river and—"

"Christina Maria. I don't want you near the river. It's dangerous. Do you hear me?"

"Aw, Mom, it's perfectly safe. All of our friends go down there, too."

"It's not safe. Some of those currents can be pretty strong." I could hear the worry in her voice. "Is everything else okay?"

"Yeah. I've even made some new friends. I went to the dance, too. I even danced with a guy. His name is Reds."

"I told you, sweetie. You're going to have a great time."

"I know." I didn't feel much like talking about all the fun I was having when she was so far away and alone, *not* having fun. "Mom?"

"Yes, honey?"

"Are you doing okay?"

"I'm fine. Please don't worry about me. Just concentrate on having a good summer, okay?"

"Okay." But I didn't want to concentrate on me when I was so worried about her. Who was going to take care of her when I was so far away? The bruises I felt inside were back and blood dry. "When can I come home?"

"Soon, honey. Soon." I heard a catch in her voice, a gasp for air. I knew she was crying. I felt sick to my stomach, just like on the day she left.

The rotten onions made my eyes burn so I closed them. I opened them a few seconds later and Uncle Butch was standing in front of me, like he was listening in on the conversation. His arms were full with a basket of clean clothes, a bar of soap, and a bottle of shampoo. A faint after-shave smell drifted in with him.

He put everything down and reached for the phone. "Don't hang up. I want to talk to her."

"Uncle Butch wants to talk to you," I said.

"Okay, put him on. Bye, honey."

"Bye, Mom." Those two little words sounded so permanent, and I felt lost and alone. After I handed him the phone I sat down at the kitchen table.

"So, tell me about Peter. Have you heard from him?" Uncle Butch asked.

My ears perked up. But Mom called my dad Pete, not Peter, so it sounded strange to me. One of my mom's favorite expressions was "Oh for Pete's sake." When I was little, I always thought she was talking about my dad. I was so naive.

"Divorce?" my uncle shook his head and turned away from me, lowering his voice, but I still heard. "We don't come from a family that gets divorced. Mama drilled that into us. No divorces in the Morgan family. Besides, I never trusted that man . . . moving you so far away from family . . ."

Wait . . . What? I've never heard her use the D word before. My heart started beating fast. Why didn't Mom tell me he called!

I was mad.

I was scared.

What would happen to us now? Now that she knew for sure that he was never coming back. That was her last hope. Jesus, Mary, and Joseph. What was going to happen next? I really needed to get back home to her.

A few minutes later, Uncle Butch hung up and turned to me. "I guess you heard."

"Yeah, I heard."

"I'm sorry. It's not the end of the world though."

Maybe not for him, but it was for me and Mom. My throat squeezed and made my voice crack. "I need to talk to my mom again." My heart was breaking, just like my family was. I tried to hold back the tears, get rid of the lump in my throat.

I got up from the table and walked toward the phone. But Uncle Butch blocked me with his arms. I tried to get around him, but he folded his arms around me in a huge bear hug. I tried again to get away, but it was like a freight train was in my path.

"I don't think that's a good idea. She's going through a hard time right now."

"But, I need to talk to her." My body tensed. I was sobbing so hard that my body was shaking. "Right now!"

He hugged me tighter, trying to keep me together, but it felt like he was squeezing the life right out of me.

"Calm down, everything will be okay."

"No, it won't!" I said, crying into his chest.

Wendy walked in. "What's the matter?"

He finally let me out of his bear grip. "Chris just found out her dad wants a divorce. She's just a little upset, that's all."

That's all! He said it so nonchalantly. My whole life was falling apart. I had just been abandoned by both my parents and he thinks I'm just a *little* upset!

"I'm sorry, Chris. But I'm glad you're here. Maybe I can help you take your mind off of everything," Wendy said sisterly. I unclenched my teeth.

I thought of my friend Lisa back home. Since my family didn't go to church, I didn't know much about religion, so when Lisa talked about God, I listened. She was the most religious person I knew. She once told me that God never dealt you more than you could handle. Now that my parents were getting a divorce and I was so far away from home, I disagreed.

CHAPTER SIX
THE GARDEN

I WOKE UP the next morning and the sun was painting the entire room yellow. I flipped on my side to face the wall and I buried my face in the pillow to block out the light. I didn't feel yellow, I felt black, like my heart.

It would be another week before I could talk to Mom. I thought about her last words to me before she drove away: "Be brave." So that's exactly what I did. I got up and faced the day, knowing I was one day closer to getting home.

Since it was Sunday and my aunt and uncle were home, we didn't dare chance going to the river. Besides, it seemed like we were just one step ahead from getting in trouble. Everything we did was against the rules. So instead of going to the river, we decided to go to Crazy Mary's house to visit the cats again.

After lunch, we packed a baggie full of leftovers for the cats to bribe them out of their hiding places.

I wanted to do something nice for Crazy Mary, so I looked around the yard and my breath caught when I saw the deep purple pansies swaying in the breeze. I walked over to Aunt Lori's flowerbed and brushed my hand over the velvety flowers. They were perfect. They were pretty and they were also my favorite color. I knew I had to share them.

I plunged my fingers underneath a bunch of pansies and scooped them up. The earth felt cool and damp. I put them in an empty flower pot lying on its side next to the garden. As I scooped up another bunch, my finger caught the edge of something sharp, and I jerked away quickly. A tiny line of blood spiraled down my pinkie. I looked at the hole where the flowers had been and saw something reflecting the sun.

"Look at that," I said, digging out the flash of light with my fingers.

"What are you doing?" Wendy asked.

"Looks like I'm digging up glass." Another piece sparkled, and I plucked it from the earth with a trowel that lay beside the garden. "Look at this. It's a bottle." I could barely make out the label of the clear broken bottle, but I could tell it was whiskey. I tossed it aside and covered the hole I had just made with some soil from around the other flowers. No one could even tell where I'd dug.

We got to Crazy Mary's house, and I took the flower pot full of pansies up the steps to the cement containers. Wendy waited on the road while Paige followed me. It felt weird being all the way up on the porch, but I had an important mission to do. I was just a few feet away from the door where I had last seen Crazy Mary, and I moved with caution. I put the flowers down and turned my attention to the two containers on either side of the porch. I pulled and tugged at the weeds, but they resisted my efforts. They had lived in those pots a long time.

Finally, I got the weeds out and dug a hole in the dirt with my hands. Then I placed the pansies in the hole and spread the dirt back around them. I looked at my handiwork. It sure did spruce up the place. I thought it was the least I could do for Crazy Mary since she was letting us visit the cats.

Mom loved flowers and each spring, we planted pansies in our front yard. I missed doing that with her. She would call what I did a "good deed," so I felt a little better about all the Rule Breaking I had been doing. I hated disappointing her. I couldn't wait to talk to her again and tell her all about Crazy Mary and Oreo.

My hands were filthy, so I rubbed them on my shorts to wipe the dirt away, but that didn't do much good. Who was I fooling anyway? There were the girls like me, and then there were girls like Julie. I was never a painted nails kind of girl.

I didn't want to ruin the moment by staying too long, so I turned to Paige and said, "Let's get out of here."

The door cracked open with a swoop. Crazy Mary peeked out from behind the door that separated her from the world. The fragrance of lilac swept out. She was the most dignified woman I had ever seen. She was carrying a tray with three glasses on it. "Would you like some lemonade?" Her voice was like baby oil. Clear and smooth.

Well, this was a shock. Not wanting to be rude, I said, "That would be great, thank you."

I walked toward Crazy Mary and took a glass of lemonade. I reached my hand out but I saw how dirty it was and pulled it back quickly.

"There's no shame in dirty hands," she said kindly. "It shows that you're a gardener. A friend to Mother Earth." She was taller than I had imagined, and thinner, but not in a frail way. She placed the tray on the porch rail.

I picked up a glass. "Thank you."

"How about you, sweetie?" she asked Paige. "You want some lemonade?"

"Yes, ma'am." Paige picked up a glass and smiled big, pushing her tongue through her missing front teeth, and then took a big sip. "Thank you."

"What about your friend over there?" she asked, pointing to where Wendy stood motionless.

"I don't think she wants any," I said, sipping on my drink. "She's my cousin Wendy." I touched Paige's shoulder. "And this is my cousin Paige."

She narrowed her eyes at me. "You're new around these parts."

"Yeah. I'm here visiting my family."

"So, Butch Morgan is your uncle?"

"Yeah," I said shyly.

She nodded. "The flowers sure do look pretty. Thank you. It's been a long while since I've had visitors."

I drank my lemonade.

"I notice that you come most days to feed the cats."

I got excited. "I named the kitten Oreo."

"Oreo? Good name. A good solid name." She smiled a wide smile and adjusted the shawl draped over her shoulders. She pushed back a loose strand of her hair.

"And I named his mother Midnight."

"Midnight is a good name for her. When she hides under the porch she is hard to find. She just came back from the vet."

"What happened to her?" I asked, concerned.

"Oh nothing, honey. I just didn't want her to have any more kittens. I try to keep up with as many of these strays as I can. When I can get a hold of them, I call someone from the local vet to come get them to be spayed or neutered. Midnight, as you call her, had eluded my grasp for some time."

"Oh, good. I'm glad nothing's wrong with her." I finished my lemonade and put the empty glass on the tray. "Thank you, Cra —uh . . ."

"I'm Mrs. Weaver. And you're welcome, my dears. Don't be strangers, hear?"

"Okay, Mrs. Weaver," I said.

I took Paige's hand and we walked down the steps together. I looked back and waved goodbye and then she disappeared back inside the house. I knew then that she wasn't crazy after all, and couldn't wait to rub it into Wendy's nose.

DINNER WAS A testament to Aunt Lori's good cooking and we ate heartily. After my dad left, Mom didn't cook much, so Aunt Lori's home cooking was a welcome change.

"How was your day, girls?" Uncle Butch asked. He slurped coffee from his "World's Best Dad" mug.

"Fine," I said and took a bite of mashed potatoes and gravy.

"Chris dug up a broken whiskey bottle from the garden," Paige tattled.

Uncle Butch chuckled. "Yeah?"

"I think it was a whiskey bottle," I said.

"That sounds about right, Chris. You have just discovered your grandfather's secret whiskey garden." Uncle Butch shoved in a big forkful of meat.

"Did Grandpa grow whiskey?" Paige asked with amazement. It was cute. I didn't need to wonder if I was that naive when I was six. I knew I was.

"No, Paige, you can't grow whiskey in a garden," Wendy said, looking at her dad for reassurance.

"That, my dear, is true. You can't grow whiskey in a garden. A whiskey garden is just a garden your grandfather created. Whenever he wanted to drink, he would tell your grandmother that he was going to work out in the garden. Instead, he went outside to sneak a drink because Grandma didn't allow any spirits in her house. To hide the evidence, he buried his bottles in the yard."

"Did Grandma ever find out?" I asked.

"I think she turned a blind eye on a lot of things that went on in those days. She was a peacekeeper, not a fighter," Aunt Lori said.

I couldn't wait to tell Mom how much I'd been learning about my relatives. I'm not sure if she was going to like what I was finding out.

"Did my mom know?" I asked. I had never seen her take a drink.

Before Uncle Butch could answer, Bob came banging out of his cottage with a beer in hand. "Hey, Butch, hey girls," he said, walking up to the screen porch.

"Hey, Bob," Uncle Butch said, pushing his plate away. He went to the refrigerator and got a beer, then grabbed his cigarettes from the table and met Bob outside.

We left them to their secret gardens and cleared the table. Without him in the cottage, I relaxed. I liked being part of the women with my cousins and aunt. I liked being part of something separate from my uncle and his gruff, overbearing presence. When he was around, he smelled hot, like sweat, and now beside Aunt Lori, I smelled the coolness of her, like lavender.

After he left, Aunt Lori hugged my cousins. She always seemed to be touching them lovingly, making sure they were okay. Then she looked at me and opened her arms. I walked over to her and tucked myself into her embrace, taking to her like a baby bird taking to a worm. I felt safe in her arms. She was as light as Uncle Butch was dark. I wanted to borrow her angel's wings and fly away home.

CHAPTER SEVEN
KING OF THE MOUNTAIN

MONDAY MORNING ARRIVED with a surprise after breakfast. While we were on the porch, Reds and Owl showed up. I looked around for Julie, but she was missing in action. It was just the two of them, so things were looking up. They both had a towel thrown over their bare shoulders and wore bathing suits. Owl raised his hand in a meek attempt to wave.

"Hey," Reds said. "Want to go to the pool with us? It's opening day."

"I guess so," Wendy said.

"You won't even have to swim with the fish," Owl said.

I chuckled. I hardly ever heard Owl speak.

"Yeah, but is it okay with your mom?" I asked her.

"Mom?" Wendy yelled to Aunt Lori, who was in the kitchen.

After a few seconds she appeared on the porch and noticed Reds and Owl standing outside. "Oh, hello, boys."

"Hi, Mrs. Morgan," they chimed.

"They want to know if we can go to the pool with them," Wendy said.

"Well, I guess it will be okay," Aunt Lori said and disappeared back inside the cottage.

"Okay," Wendy said to the guys, "but we have to get our bathing suits on first. It might take a few minutes."

"We'll wait," Reds said.

My stomach curled up inside me. Just us and the guys? No Julie? What a nice turn of events.

We were in the bedroom changing into our suits as fast as possible. Paige walked in and started changing too.

"Where do you think you're going?" Wendy asked.

"To the pool, like you guys."

"No you're not. Mom, tell Paige she can't come with us. Please?"

Paige started to argue so Aunt Lori came into the bedroom. "It's okay, Paige. The girls want to go by themselves." She winked at us.

Paige jutted her bottom lip out at her mom with her hands on her hips. I don't know where she studied the craft of manipulation, but she sure was good at it. I was beginning to learn a thing or two from her.

"Okay, honey, give me fifteen minutes and I'll take you to the pool when I finish hanging the laundry on the line."

That seemed to be a solution we could all live with. Then I realized that I hadn't shaved my legs since I arrived and they were hairy.

"I've got to shave my legs," I told Wendy and went to the shower to find the razor. I let the water run down my legs, soaped up, and quickly ran the razor over them. Afterward, I threw shorts on over my bathing suit, and we were ready to go.

I walked next to Reds while Wendy and Owl followed. Without Julie around, the sun seemed brighter and my steps seemed lighter somehow.

"My older brother is working at Coney Island this summer and he'll be able to get us in at a discount. Isn't that cool?" Reds said.

"Yeah," I said.

I wonder if he meant just the four of us. I was nervous because I never talked to Reds alone, without Julie around, or loud music playing. I wasn't the best at making small talk. That's why I liked having Lisa around back home because she loved to talk. She seemed to fill in all the silent moments with her constant chatter.

"I want to ride the roller coaster," Owls said, punching Reds' shoulder lightly.

"Me, too," Wendy said.

As we approached the pool, I could hear screams of excitement and splashing. I looked at Wendy and smiled, but my smile faded as we walked through the gate. Sitting on the life guard stand was Julie. She was wearing a one piece red bathing suit with a whistle around her neck. She was tan, and her red nails matched her suit. She was a queen on her throne and we were her loyal subjects. She had so much confidence up there. She saw me looking at her and waved but her heart wasn't in it. I waved back half-heartedly.

"Oh, great," I said to Wendy under my breath so the guys wouldn't hear. "She's the lifeguard? And she made me swim out to Slippery Rock and watched as I almost drowned! What a—" My voice got louder and Reds overheard me.

"Well, she's not really the lifeguard. Yet, anyway. She's the lifeguard's assistant until she's old enough. Her mother has some pull with the homeowners association, so . . . that's how she got the job." Reds pointed to the real lifeguard who was just emerging from the pool house. She had a water testing kit in her hand. She was also wearing a red one piece bathing suit.

"Look, it's Tommy and Freckles," Owl said.

They were in the pool, waving to us. We waved back, but my eyes were focused on Julie. We picked out a spot by the pool to lay our towels down. It was packed, just like at the dance. I felt self-conscious and didn't want to take my shorts off.

"Come on, Chris, what are you waiting for?" Reds asked as he got in the pool.

I slipped off my shorts quickly and got in the pool as fast as I could. Once submerged in the water, I felt better. A few minutes later, we made our way over to Tommy and Freckles. The water was cold, and I bent my knees so that I was covered up to my shoulders. I hoped my headlights weren't showing.

We splashed in the water for about fifteen minutes. Slowly I lost my inhibitions and warmed up. I felt safe in the water and missed my swim team, missed my friend, Lisa, who was on the swim team with me.

"Come on, get on my shoulders. We're going to play King of the Mountain," Reds said to me. "We challenge you and Wendy to a battle," he said to Owl.

"We accept," Owl said.

The guys went underwater and we climbed on their shoulders. Up on top of Reds' shoulders, I felt exposed again, uncomfortable. My legs were intertwined with his arms, skin against skin. I could feel his strength as he held me up on my own throne. I was glad that my legs were shaved.

Reds caressed my thighs then, and I smiled my shit-eating grin at Julie. My mom told me not to cuss, but my dad used the term, and I liked it, so I kept it in my vocabulary. It was one of the few things I had left of him.

In an instant, Wendy had her hands on me, trying to knock me off Reds' shoulders. I fought back. It was a balancing act. When I leaned too far to the right, Reds' leaned to the left. It was hard to balance because there was nothing for me to hold on to, unless I wrapped an arm around Reds' head and risked the chance that he wouldn't be able to see. He held me tight around my thighs and it felt good to be tangled up with him, my legs tucked around his arms and my feet on his back. I wasn't even worried about my headlights showing anymore.

As we played, I saw Aunt Lori arrive with Paige. She took a lounge chair next to Alice. Paige joined us in the water. Soon, a black-haired girl showed up too and got on top of Freckles' shoulders when he went underwater.

"Paige, come here. You can get on my shoulders," Tommy said. Julie watched closely as Paige wrapped her legs around Tommy's shoulders.

Once we were all partnered up, we started to knock each other off our partners' shoulders. The last one on top won the game and I was trying my best to knock the black-haired girl down. Julie was fidgeting, trying not to notice us, but I caught her looking at us every chance she got.

I knocked the black-haired girl off Freckles' shoulders first. Next to go was Wendy. Now it was me and Reds against Tommy and Paige. For being so little, Paige was quick, and we wrestled for a long while. Tommy was taller than Reds, but Paige was shorter than me, so we balanced out pretty fairly. Tommy definitely had more muscles, but I didn't want to be on his shoulders. I was right where I wanted to be.

To win the game, I made a drastic move and put my foot in Tommy's face so he couldn't see, and then I knocked Paige off her lofty position.

"We won!" I raised my hands in victory.

Reds went underwater so I could get off his shoulders. He resurfaced and had a smile I hadn't seen before. He was triumphant and happy. He held up his hands to me and I high fived him, smiling back. Then he put his fingers in between mine so that our hands were intertwined. Nice move. I was excited and scared at the same time. I felt his boney fingers pressing against my own. I couldn't wait to tell Lisa back home. We often talked about what it would be like to have our first boyfriend.

As we were celebrating and splashing each other, Tommy came over and high fived Reds, then me. "Good game."

I was now the queen and there was nothing Julie could do about it. Or so I thought.

The whistle blew long and hard. All eyes turned to Julie. "Adult swim."

Well done, worthy opponent.

CHAPTER EIGHT
FALLING

THE NEXT MORNING, we turned on the radio. We were dancing around like jerks when Reds and Owl showed up again. Embarrassed, I walked over to the screen where they were. Wendy followed me, hiding her hairbrush microphone.

"Hi, Chris. Hi, Wendy. Guess what? I got four tickets to Coney Island! Do you guys want to go with us?" Reds said. "My brother said he would drive us. He has to work anyway."

"Yes," I said immediately.

Wendy let out a little squeal. "I have to ask my mom." She went in to the kitchen to ask Aunt Lori.

I could hear her from where I was on the porch.

"Mom, the guys want to know if we can go to Coney Island with them. Can we, Mom, please?"

"I don't know. How are you going to get there?"

"Reds' brother is going to take us," Wendy said.

"Reds? Who's Reds?" Aunt Lori asked.

"I mean, Dave."

"Is that the Johnson boy?"

"Yeah, Dave, the Johnson boy."

"I know his mother. She's real nice."

"Get with the program, Mom. We went with them to the pool yesterday." I could hear Wendy's growing frustration.

"I don't know, honey. I should really talk to your father first."

"Oh please, Mom," Wendy said.

I imagined her on her knees with her hands pressed together in front of her face as if in prayer. A few seconds passed and I realized in that short span of time I was holding my breath. I looked at the guys and they were smiling at me, expectantly.

Aunt Lori walked in with Paige following closely behind her.

"Hi, boys," Aunt Lori said.

"Hi, Mrs. Morgan," Reds said.

There was an uncomfortable silence.

"Okay. I guess it will be all right," Aunt Lori finally said.

I let out my breath.

"What about me? Can I go too?" Paige asked.

"No, honey. This is just for the older girls."

"Aw, Mom. I want to go too."

Aunt Lori rubbed the top of her head. "We'll do something fun together today, okay? Promise."

"We can go!" Wendy said, but I didn't know why since we all heard Aunt Lori say we could.

"Okay, great. I'll go tell my brother and we'll pick you up in fifteen minutes," Reds said.

ONCE WE WERE inside the amusement park, we made a beeline for the rides and of course our first ride was the roller coaster. We sat behind Wendy and Owl. I was so excited I wanted to scream. The anticipation was getting the best of me. The seat was small, forcing us to sit close together. Reds pushed his hairy bare leg against mine. He leaned his upper body into mine to talk so I could hear over all the noise. He was gentle and attentive. I had never known that kind of sweetness before.

I heard a loud clank as we began the slow climb up the incline. There was a constant rattling as the chain pulled us to the top. We tipped downward and began our descent. I squeezed my hands tighter around the bar in front of us. I was as scared as I had been swimming in the river my first day of summer vacation. But this time I had someone by my side, and I felt reassured.

I leaned into Reds and he leaned back as if we were the only two people in the world, clinging on to some unknown emotion. I felt myself falling as we headed down the hill. I had a hard time breathing as we slammed against each other on the twists and turns. I felt myself opening up to him.

When the ride was over, we went over to the Ferris wheel and waited our turn in the heat of the day.

The operator swung the bar open and I climbed in on the seat next to Reds. The bar swung closed, trapping us for the duration of the ride. Next, Owl and Wendy got on, and we stopped several more times as riders loaded. Slowly the wheel moved up toward the sky until we were on the very top waiting for the ride to start. My heart quickened at how high we were.

"Do you want to go be my girlfriend?" Reds asked me.

Of course I did. I'd never had a boyfriend. But I hesitated for a second.

He nudged me. "Well?"

"Sure." Who else would I date?

"Okay." He leaned into me and kissed me. It was as if our breathing was the only sound. He gently offered his tongue and waited with anticipation. I offered my tongue back to him but I was scared. It didn't taste like the cigarettes and whiskey from our first kiss.

A smile permanently took up residence on my face and I looked out at the vast land around us. The amusement park was lush and green. Flowers planted in mulch beds were so thick that I could smell the sweetness of their blooms even on top of the Ferris wheel. The leaves on the trees were so full that I couldn't see through them, even when the warm breeze rustled through them. Everything was in bloom, including me, and I felt as if there was a waking up inside, as though I'd been asleep my whole life.

WHEN WE GOT back to the cottage, I pulled Wendy into the bedroom. "Guess what?"

"What?"

"Reds asked me to be his girlfriend!"

Wendy let out a little squeal. "Oh my God. What did you say?"

"I said yes, of course."

"I can't believe it. You're so lucky."

Paige came into the room then, singing. "Chris and Reds, sitting in a tree. K-i-s-s-i-n-g. First comes love, then comes marriage . . ."

"Cut it out, Paige," Wendy said. "You're always spying on us. I'm telling Mom, you little brat."

"I'm not a brat," Paige said.

"Are too," Wendy said.

"Oh come on, y'all. No fighting, okay?" I said. I was too happy to let them ruin my mood.

Wendy leaned down and got in Paige's face. "Just don't go running your mouth about this to Mom and Dad, got it?"

"Got it." Paige shrugged.

But she didn't get it. As soon as Uncle Butch got home from work and before he could even sit down, Paige was at his side.

"Guess what, Daddy?"

"What?"

"Wendy and Chris got to go to Coney Island with Reds and Owl."

"Is that right?" Uncle Butch said. He seemed concerned.

"They wouldn't let me go, either," Paige said.

Aunt Lori came onto the porch where we were. "Did you have a good day at work, honey?"

"Yeah, but what is this about the girls going to Coney Island?"

"The guys invited them and I let them go."

"Alone?" His voice shot up a bit.

"No. Dave's brother took them."

"Was he at the park with them?"

"Yeah. He works there," Aunt Lori said.

"So really, no supervision, right?" He seemed angry.

"And Chris is Reds' girlfriend," Paige said. I liked Paige, but she sure was a tattle-tale.

"Who the hell is Reds?" Uncle Butch asked, confused.

"Reds is Dave. It's his nickname on account of him always wearing his Cincinnati Reds baseball cap . . ." Wendy said.

"I don't care who he is!" Uncle Butch's face turned red. He was doing that a lot lately. "Aren't you girls a little young to be dating?"

"No," Wendy said.

I was silent.

He wiggled his big sausage finger between me and Wendy. "I don't want you two hanging out with those boys any more. It doesn't look right for such young girls to be around older boys."

"They're only a year older," Wendy said.

"Oh, honey. Let the girls be. They're just having fun with their friends. It's all innocent," Aunt Lori said.

"Yeah, well, it's all innocent until it's not," Uncle Butch said. "Boys that age only have one thing on their mind, and I don't like them hanging around with them unsupervised!"

He went to the kitchen and grabbed a beer from the fridge. The screen door banged as he left.

Wendy and I exchanged looks, and smiled. Even Uncle Butch's bad mood couldn't spoil our perfect day.

CHAPTER NINE
MAKE OVER

IT WAS FRIDAY and I was excited not only because of the dance, but because I could call my mom tomorrow. It had been a week since my phone call to her and boy oh boy, I really needed to talk to her.

After lunch, Paige went over to Cody and Callie's cottage next door, and we left her there playing with her friends. Then we walked down to the river to meet up with the gang.

On the way I asked, "What do you think about Freckles?"

"Do you like him?" Wendy seemed surprised.

"No!" I said. "He just seems like a bully."

"Oh, don't worry about him, he's sweet as pie. But his daddy's meaner than a snake." Wendy bent down and picked up a stick. "His dad was in the Vietnam war. When he got back from the war, he wasn't right in the head. He mostly stays inside his cottage and drinks all day. He doesn't work anymore, either. He's a loner. Freckles' mom died giving birth to him so it's only Freckles and his dad, and his dad is very strict on him. That's why he has a crew cut. His dad made him cut off all his hair. I think it makes Freckles feel good to always be in charge of things, you know, like getting the cigarettes and whiskey."

We reached the river's edge, and they were all there. We sat around on logs in the clearing, talking, but the camera of my memory was flashing back to last Saturday when I had talked to my mom. I missed her and Lisa, and couldn't wait to see them again.

"Hey, Chris, what the heck?" Reds startled me out of my thoughts. "Check your butt."

Reds and I were sitting side by side on a damp log, our shoulders touching. I liked the way his dark hair curled in different directions around his face.

I stood up and looked behind me. "Why? What is it?" I swiped my hand across my butt, looking over my shoulder to see what he was talking about.

"Not that." He laughed. "I was talking about your cigarette."

I had let it burn down without touching it to my mouth. "Oh, thanks." I smiled at him, feeling stupid. I crushed the cigarette into the mud with my foot and then sat back down next to him. I thought about my grandpa's throat cancer. I pictured it as a big lump of black tar blocking his vocal cords, trapping him inside his mind with no way to speak. It seemed stupid to smoke, knowing that it could cause cancer.

"I don't really like smoking," I said to Reds, but Julie, who was just a few feet away, overheard me.

"What?" Julie asked.

My face started to burn. "I said, I don't like smoking."

"Well, well, New Girl is a goody-two-shoes."

"No, I'm not. I just don't like smoking." I stared at her, my anger rising. I was doing everything she expected me to do to be part of the group, but I was getting fed up. "And stop calling me New Girl, my name is Chris."

"Calm down, New Girl. You don't have to be so touchy." She clucked her tongue on the roof of her mouth and went back to talking to Tommy. Everyone else stopped looking at me too and continued with their conversations.

"Wendy and Owl are cute together, don't you think?" I said, trying to break the tension.

"Yeah, I guess." Reds shrugged.

I reached in my pocket and pulled the penny out that my mom gave me. I rubbed its smooth surface with my thumb and index finger. I did it so often I didn't even think about it anymore.

"What's that?" Reds asked.

"It's a penny," I said.

"What? It doesn't look like a penny," Reds said, unimpressed.

"Well, no. Not anymore. But it used to be a penny. Now it's something else I guess."

"It's worthless."

I quickly put the penny back in my pocket and changed the subject.

"Does Freckles have a girlfriend?" I thought about the black-haired girl at the pool.

"No. Says he wouldn't want to be with just one girl, but maybe he just feels like the girls are too young for him here. He's fifteen, you know."

"Fifteen!"

"Yeah, he failed a grade, but we still hang out."

"What's Tommy's story?" I asked.

"Nothing. Just your typical all-American boy. He plays for the football team during the school year. He's had a crush on Julie ever since I can remember."

"What are you two whispering about over there?" Julie asked, walking toward us.

"Nothing," I said.

She was pretty, I'll give her that, but I looked at her feet, and they had mud on them just like the rest of us, and her painted toenails, well; they just looked like drops of blood in the earth.

Tommy followed her and put his hands around her waist from behind. She leaned back into him; her head nestled against his neck. Then she turned toward him and they embraced, his hands around her waist and her hands around his neck. There wasn't any sunlight between them as they kissed, long and hard. It was a private moment and I looked away.

After a minute, Reds shuffled his feet and stood up. "Ahem."

"Oh, sorry, we got carried away, I guess," Julie said proudly. She was claiming her territory and we all knew it.

I stood up next to Reds and reached for his hand. I didn't have painted toenails, but I had a winning smile, and I used it on Reds. He took my hand. Julie wasn't the be-all and know-all that she thought she was.

I looked at Julie. I wonder if she was getting my anti-Julie vibe because just then she walked over to me.

"What?" I said.

She touched my hair.

"Hey, New Girl. Why do you always wear your hair up?"

"I don't know. It's easier than wearing it down, I guess."

"You and Wendy are coming with me." That was definitely an order.

"Why?" Wendy asked.

"Come on. Follow me. We are going to have a make-over at my place."

We said bye to the guys and followed Julie up the path. Once clear, we headed toward the pavilion with Julie leading the way.

A few minutes later, we turned down the dirt road toward the playground. Julie's cottage was the second one on the right.

Julie burst through the screen door. We followed.

She stopped at the entrance to the living room. "Mom, I'm home."

Her mother was in a chair, facing the TV.

"I got a couple of friends over," Julie said.

She didn't turn around to greet us. She just continued to watch TV. "Okay, honey."

Julie flopped down on the edge of her bed and Wendy sat beside her. I sat on the chair at her desk, looking into the mirror above it. Makeup was scattered over the top of it. I had never seen so much makeup in my life! No wonder Julie always looked so good.

There was a poster over her bed. It was a kitten holding onto a tree branch. On the bottom of the poster it said, "Hang in There Baby."

Julie walked over to her record player and put a forty five on the turntable. I watched the warped record spin and the needle rode the grooves like a car over a hill. I always thought that music breathed life. The beautiful notes mixed with the emotion of the singer could change a mood so fast that the sun and rain would harmonize, giving birth to rainbows.

Her bedroom was painted light blue and her bedspread and curtains were white with yellow flowers on them. There were also splashes of tiny purple flowers here and there. I envied her delicate, feminine surroundings. Everything but the makeup was put neatly in its place. At my house, we were clean, but not everything was in its place.

"My mom is always in front of the TV, watching her soap operas," Julie said quietly. "I don't even think she knows where I am half of the time and the other half, she just doesn't care. Like I'm invisible." There was a sadness in her voice. Her mom was so far away, even in the same house. My mom was two states away and I still felt close to her. I felt bad for Julie.

She shrugged and came up behind me and plugged in a curling iron. "First, we're going to do your makeup." She turned the chair so I was facing her. She reached over to the messy pile of makeup and picked up the mascara. A few quick swipes of the wand on my eyelashes, and wa-la, my eyes looked brighter and bigger somehow. Next, she patted a brush over the powder foundation and applied it all over my face. Bold brush strokes over and over, like I was a picture she was painting.

"Purse your lips," Julie said.

"What?"

"You know. Pucker. Like you're going to kiss someone."

"Pretend you're going to kiss Reds," Wendy said.

I puckered my lips and Julie applied lipstick like she had been doing this her entire life. She reached into her makeup pile and grabbed some blush, which she applied to my cheeks.

"That looks good on you, Chris." Wendy picked up the blue eye shadow and turned it over in her hand, examining it like she was a scientist. "Here, do this next." She handed the eye shadow to Julie.

I tried to see myself in the mirror again, but as I turned my head toward the mirror, Julie put her hand on my face, forcing me to look back at her. "No. Not yet. Not until I'm finished with you."

"Okay, okay," I said. "Jeez."

"Close your eyes."

I closed them and Julie started with my right eye, applying the eye shadow. It tickled, but it felt good too. I felt important. Like I was finally someone other than "The Loser" me that existed back in Virginia.

After she finished with my left eye, she said, "Okay, you can open your eyes now, but don't look in the mirror yet."

"Okay, but I can't wait to see it," I said.

"Next, we're going to curl your hair." Julie took the elastic band from my hair and ran her fingers through it to fluff it out.

Wendy busied herself by looking through all the makeup while Julie curled my hair.

After a few minutes, Julie said, "Okay, you can look now."

I turned the chair and looked in the mirror. I was surprised. Amazed. My face seemed softer. All of my red splotches were now invisible. I looked at all the colors on my face and I really did feel like I was a painting. I had transformed from the awkward Skipper doll into the beautiful Barbie doll."

"Wow. I can't believe it."

"I know," Julie said. "That's how I felt the first time I wore makeup. You feel different huh?" She paused. "You get noticed."

That seemed like a strange thing to say about makeup. I wonder if she started to wear makeup to get the attention she seemed to love so much. Then I thought about what she said about her mother, and how invisible her mom made her feel.

Maybe she just wanted to be noticed by her mother. I was beginning to understand Julie a little.

"You look great, Chris," Wendy said.

"Yep. Reds will really notice you now," Julie said. She turned to Wendy. "Now it's your turn."

CHAPTER TEN
DANCING THE NIGHT AWAY

AFTER JULIE FINISHED Wendy's makeup we headed back to the cottage. Excitement welled in my heart and threatened to burst out. Wendy talked me into painting my fingernails, but I refused when it came to painting my toenails like Julie's. My toes weren't the prettiest of things and that would just draw too much attention to them. At least I didn't have dirt caked under my nails anymore. Wendy talked me into discarding my tomboy clothes and into wearing one of her dresses. With my makeup, dress, and painted fingernails, I felt grown up.

When Uncle Butch saw us, he smiled so big I thought his cheeks were going to fall off of the sides of his face.

"Well, don't you two young ladies look nice," he said.

Wendy did a little bow. "Thanks, Dad. Julie did our hair and makeup."

As Wendy bent over to take her bow, he looked directly at me.

"So pretty, too!"

I don't think he meant to emphasize the word, "pretty" so much, but that's how it came out.

"Aw, Dad," Wendy said, brushing the compliment away.

Aunt Lori came onto the porch. Paige followed behind. They were also wearing dresses.

"Well, look at us girls. We're all dressed up and ready for the dance," Aunt Lori said.

We walked with Uncle Butch, Aunt Lori, and Paige, but planned to spend the evening with the gang.

On our way to the pavilion, I heard the hot bugs singing their high-pitched song of summer. My feet skipped because I couldn't wait to show Reds that I had learned to dance.

Uncle Butch put his bottle, wrapped in a brown paper bag, on the table. "Wendy, go get us some pop and ice, please." He handed her money and we headed for the snack bar.

I looked for Julie and the guys as people spilled into the pavilion, but they were nowhere to be found. "Wendy, do you see them?"

She scanned the place. "No," she said, disappointed.

She kept her eyes on the picnic table we had claimed for ourselves last Friday and would claim again tonight. That seemed to hold true for the adults, too. People sat at the same tables as they did last week. I imagined that they had done this for years.

We got to the snack bar and waited our turn, but the teenage boy behind the counter was ignoring us. It was the same boy as last week.

"We've been here forever," Wendy said, stomping her foot.

The black-haired girl was also behind the counter. She smiled and waved to me. One pool game with Freckles and she thought she was my friend. She was going to have to go through an initiation like I had to, to be part of our group. I realized then that I was becoming as stuck up as Julie. I remembered Wendy's words. "Popularity changes people." She was right. I did feel different. I felt special.

"Well, don't say it too loud. He'll never wait on us," I said. "It helps if you smile and look him right in the eyes."

I was watching the back of the pavilion and noticed Julie walk up the back steps with her loyal subjects behind her. I expected to see Freckles bringing up the rear, but he was missing in action. I nudged Wendy, and she waved to them. Finally the boy behind the counter approached us.

"What'll you girls have tonight?" the boy asked.

"Two bottles of pop and two buckets of ice, please." Wendy said.

He handed us the order and we dropped off one of the bottles of Coke and a bucket of ice at Uncle Butch's table, then made our way through the growing crowd to our friends with the other bottle of Coke and bucket of ice.

"Hey," Julie said nonchalantly as we approached. Then she noticed our dresses and painted nails and smiled. She tapped my shoulder. "Hey, Chris."

"Yeah?" I said. It was the first time she called me Chris, and I finally felt like I belonged. I guess she didn't feel so threatened by me.

I never belonged in any of the *cool* groups at school. It was just me and Lisa, The Loners. I couldn't wait to tell Lisa that I was a bona fide member of the COOL group. I felt popular for the first time in my life.

"Nice." Julie was wearing a hip-hugger mini skirt and a halter top, which showed off her flat stomach. Wearing a dress was one thing, but I drew the line at showing my belly button.

Reds came over to me. "Wow, Chris, you're prit-a-ful."

"What?" Did I hear that right? He thought I was pitiful. This was a disaster.

Reds stuttered. "I mean, you look pretty. I wanted to say pretty, but I also wanted to say beautiful. Sorry. It came out wrong."

"Thanks," I said shyly. I didn't realize one little dress and some makeup would make such a big impression.

Julie leaned close to Tommy and whispered in his ear. She swiped her hair from her forehead. Then she leaned toward Wendy and whispered something I couldn't hear. Was she saying something about me?

I tugged on Wendy's dress for the translation. She obliged. "We're all going to the river after the dance. We're going to sneak out early to avoid the adults."

Our plan was to leave at seven thirty before the DJ kicked us out, and before the adults could ask us to babysit.

"Is that allowed?" I don't know why I asked. It seemed that everything we had done so far wasn't allowed, but I kept doing them anyway, like some foreigner in a new world, following blindly.

The DJ tested the microphone and the crowd quieted down. I could feel the buzz all around me like a high voltage wire, vibrating down to my bones.

Then, as if on cue, Freckles appeared at the table and touched his backpack with confidence. "I got it."

"Finally. We were afraid you would let us down," Julie said. She opened the bottle of Coke and poured it into the cups filled with ice while Freckles lowered them under the table and filled them with whiskey.

The DJ played the first song and shy looks passed between the girls and boys. The adults jockeyed for position on the dance floor. Couples were already dancing by the time Aunt Lori and Uncle Butch got on the floor, but everyone made room for them as they moved toward the center.

Our group hung at the edges for what seemed like hours but it really wasn't that long. I took a few sips of whiskey and Coke, waiting for someone to make the first move. Finally, hands connected, feet shuffled, and the old wood floor buckled and swayed underneath me. Julie and Tommy made the first move, which didn't surprise me. Julie loved the attention and Tommy liked pleasing Julie. Owl and Wendy slipped in beside them, dancing the swing like everyone else. I'm glad Aunt Lori and Uncle Butch had given us dance lessons.

A few sips later, Reds put his drink down and innocently tucked his hand into mine. He took my drink from my hand and coaxed me onto the dance floor. As we were dancing, I felt the sweat under my arms, and my footwork was jumbling together.

"Just relax and follow my lead," Reds yelled over the music.

The music was intoxicating, or maybe it was the whiskey, I couldn't tell and didn't care. Then something extraordinary happened. I relaxed and remembered the dance lessons my aunt and uncle had given us. I couldn't dance particularly well, but I could follow easy enough. Excitement raced through my veins, and I smiled at the concept of having a boyfriend. Everything was so new to me, like the sparkling stars I saw on the river my first day.

By the end of the dance, everyone had paired up the same as last Friday night. Reds pointed to Freckles, who was standing by the black-haired girl in the corner. Then he grabbed my hand and led me off the dance floor to them.

"Hey, man, what's up? We're ready for another drink. How about you?" Reds asked.

"Been ready," Freckles said.

"I'll pour the pop and you take it from there," Reds said.

"Cool." Freckles was a soul of few words. Owl and Wendy soon joined us.

We finished our drinks and as the night continued, we got louder and my head got lighter. We were all dancing together in a circle, each one of us doing our own thing. I liked dancing with a partner, but this was fun too. The music felt like it was coursing through my veins, banging in my heart. Suddenly I was in the middle of the circle. I had become like Julie after all, and I felt like the queen of the dance. When the DJ played a Roy Orbison's song I started to sing to the words, and pretty soon, I felt both pretty and like a woman. I was twirling and moving and raised my hands up to the ceiling.

There were other kids at the dance, but they remained on the outskirts because we were the popular group. We were The Untouchables. I had arrived!

Julie tapped my shoulder. "Okay, dancing queen. Let's go."

I looked over at Aunt Lori and Uncle Butch to see if they were paying attention to us, but they were too busy dancing to notice us.

One by one we left and waited until the last person was safely out of sight before we headed to the river. The moon was high and bright and the night air was hot and humid. I felt perspiration bead down my back. It was hard to breathe. Julie, who was walking next to Tommy, didn't seem to sweat like I did, she glistened. But Wendy looked as hot as I felt, and the guys all had wet spots under their arms and down their backs.

Freckles pulled a flashlight out of his backpack and led the way. After a few minutes, we reached the top of the path and started down single file.

"Snake," Freckles said.

I jumped back, my happy feeling gone. "What? I hate snakes!" I looked down the path and sure enough, there it was in the middle of the path, its head reared up, warning us to keep back. "I'm not going down there."

My eyes adjusted in the moonlight. Reds walked toward it.

"Chris, it won't hurt you, it's just a harmless little snake." He gently grabbed it around the head and held it up, its body curling around his arm. He was a magic snake charmer, and he carefully placed the snake off to the side of the path. It quickly disappeared into the brush. "It's not even poisonous." He was gentle with the snake and I knew I could trust him, just like I instinctively knew I could trust Crazy Mary.

"What did you do that for?" Freckles asked, producing a pocket knife from his jeans. "We could have cut its head off and watched it squirm."

I furrowed my brow at him.

"Put that knife away before you cut yourself," Julie said.

"Come on," Reds said to me.

"I don't know. How do I know it's safe?" I asked.

Wendy locked elbows with me. "It's safe. You can tell a poisonous snake by the shape of its head. If it has a round head like the snake on the path, it's not poisonous. But if it has a pointed head, watch out, it's poisonous. My dad taught me that."

I felt better, but I was still freaked out and didn't move. "Is that true?"

"Actually, yes," Reds said. "But a venomous snake will also have a small depression between the eye and the nostril. That's called a pit, which is used to sense heat in their prey."

He came up to me and hooked his elbow around my free one. "I'll protect you. Besides there's something I want you to see." That made me move further down the path, but I was cautious.

At the river's edge, there was a chorus of frogs, crickets, and katydids singing their summer song. The moon was floating above the trees, and the lightning bugs glowed like candles on a cake. The muddy air felt soft against my skin.

I looked around cautiously for more snakes. When I was sure there weren't any, I sat down on a log and Reds sat next to me, our bodies touching. I felt the thrill of it, thirsty for his attention.

Reds leaned into my shoulder and talked low so no one else would hear. He seemed nervous but I didn't know why. He reached for my hand. His hand was sweaty and his nervousness made me nervous. Finally he pulled something out of his pocket and handed it to me. "I made this for you."

It was a macramé bracelet with hemp twine knotted around blue beads. "Thank you," I said.

"I hope you like it."

"It's beautiful." He took the bracelet from my hand and tied it around my right wrist.

Julie twirled in the moonlight in front of Tommy. Owl was standing by Wendy with his arm on her shoulder. Freckles picked up a stone and skipped it across the water. It was peaceful for a long while, until an unfamiliar voice disrupted the night.

"What are you kids doing down there?"

We were all quiet.

"Answer me." It was a man's voice, deep and authoritative.

I stood up, stepping on a twig.

"I can hear you." We heard the man getting closer. Finally, we saw the face that went with the voice. He was a broad man with a crew cut and a square jaw.

"Dad, what are you doing down here?" Freckles asked.

"I knew you were up to no good, boy. Get your ass over here right now!"

Freckles got within arm's reach, and his dad struck him on the back of his head and shoved him up the path. Freckles stumbled to his knees. As he was getting back up, his dad kicked him in the gut. Freckles brought his legs up to his stomach, moaning.

He finally got to his feet.

His dad called him a sissy and slapped him across the face. "I knew you were stealing cigarettes and whiskey from me boy. Now get home."

Freckles didn't even look at us as he started up the path.

His dad followed him then stopped and turned around to face us. "The rest of you better get home too, before I tell your parents."

After Freckles and his dad disappeared, we gathered together like a swarm of angry, nervous bees that had been kicked out of their hive.

I couldn't believe what had just happened. "I hope Freckles is okay."

"Me too," Wendy said.

"Wow, his dad's pretty pissed off," Reds said.

"I hope he doesn't tell our parents," Owl said. "We would all be in big trouble."

"We better go," Julie said.

Wendy and I ran back to the cottage. We were in bed, pretending to be asleep when Aunt Lori and Uncle Butch got home.

I didn't know what would come next. It seemed like we were always just one step in front of getting caught. Everything I did since I arrived was breaking rules. I thought about how good I was back home. I wouldn't dare break the rules, but now I was a bona fide rebel. I just kept following Julie's lead, and her path was leading me right to Hell and further away from my mom.

CHAPTER ELEVEN
HEART OF DARKNESS

SATURDAY MORNING BROUGHT the promise of rain as the elephant gray clouds rolled in. After I got dressed, I went to the porch where Wendy and Paige were.

"Girls, set the table please," Aunt Lori said. "And Wendy, your father wants to talk to you before you leave the cottage today."

"What about?" Wendy asked, but we already knew the answer.

"About last night. You disappeared, didn't tell us where you were going, who you were with. We had to get Karen to babysit Paige and—"

Wendy cut her off. "Is Dad real mad?" I could tell she had asked this question many times before.

Aunt Lori stroked Wendy's hair and smiled sadly. "He's mad now, but by the end of the day he will calm down. Especially since I'm making his favorite cake."

I heard Uncle Butch stir in the master bedroom. "Lori, bring me some aspirin and a glass of water." His voice was slow and hoarse, and I knew from last Saturday that he was hung over. We finished breakfast without a word and went into the living room. Paige followed us and we played cards quietly. The alcohol ate at my stomach like a fungus on bread.

I felt some sort of impending doom.

Wendy whispered to me. "Don't say anything about last night. Let me do all the talking." Fear crept over me as I sensed the trouble we were in. "No matter what, don't admit to anything."

Paige looked up from her cards ready to speak, but Wendy cut her a look and stopped her from talking.

A half hour later we got bored, and Wendy and I went into the kitchen. Aunt Lori was bent over looking into the oven, checking to see if the cake was ready.

"Can we please go outside before it rains?" Wendy whispered to keep her father from hearing.

"No, he wants to talk to you before you go anywhere today. I'm sorry, but that's just the way it is." She removed the cake and put it on the counter, then flipped the dishtowel across her shoulder and swiped the loose strands of hair from her face.

We went back to the living room where Paige had set up the Monopoly Board.

"Aw, Paige, I don't want to play that," Wendy said.

"Okay, but I might slip up and tell Dad that you're keeping secrets."

"You little brat." Wendy slammed her fist down on the board, waited a minute, and then picked up the race car. "Okay, you win. Are you happy now? Forcing people to play with you."

Tears threatened Paige's eyes, and I quickly jumped in. "I like you, Paige. You're not forcing me to play with you."

Paige smiled at me and stuck her tongue out at Wendy. Trying to keep the tears from falling, I added, "Hey, y'all know that song by War?"

"What song?" Wendy counted her fake money, put it into piles by denomination, and tucked it under the game board.

"C'mon, you know." I sang the words, "Why can't we be friends . . . ?"

Paige tilted her head like a lost puppy and Wendy continued to count.

"Y'all know it." I continued to sing until they picked up the beat and the words. Singing with them actually made me feel like I truly did have sisters.

My legs were cramped so I stood up and stretched. Paige put a finger to her mouth. I heard Uncle Butch bumping around in his bedroom.

We were quiet as mice trying to avoid the mousetrap. But no matter how quiet we were, we couldn't avoid him forever. Finally, Uncle Butch appeared. He was wrapped in a white bathrobe with his bare chest and legs exposed. His wide frame blocked the doorway. "Wendy, Chris, come here. I want to talk to you."

He cleared the doorway, but only as Wendy pushed past him. I was afraid he didn't have anything on underneath his robe and I didn't want to find out. I felt awkward and hoped his belt was cinched tight enough around his waist to keep his robe closed. Paige followed us quietly into the kitchen. I didn't see Aunt Lori anywhere.

"I don't like when you disappear without telling us where you're going or who you're with. We looked all over for you two at eight, and you were nowhere to be seen."

We said nothing.

"Know what else? We didn't see any of your friends, either. You know better than that."

"I'm sorry, Dad. It won't happen again."

"You're damn right it won't. You're grounded until I tell you you're not." His voice was loud and authoritative.

"We weren't doing anything wrong, honest."

"Then why didn't you tell us where you were going?"

"Because I knew you would want me to babysit Paige and—"

"That's no excuse. I also don't want you hanging around that river, especially at night."

"We weren't down there, honest. We were in the game room."

Wendy told a boldface lie. I held my breath, not wanting to be part of it.

"Is that true?" Uncle Butch asked me.

I was still as a statue. "Yes."

"You're getting too big for your britches, young lady. From now on, you will tell us where you're going." He finished by pointing his big sausage finger at Wendy's nose, almost touching her face. He held it there for a couple of seconds, daring her to move.

She stood, unflinching, but as much as I was afraid, she was brave.

He moved his hand from her face. Only then did I breathe. Paige remained quiet.

We crept back into the living room and sat on the floor. Paige followed us. We played Monopoly until it was dinner time.

"Butch, come help me stuff the chicken with these herbs," Aunt Lori called from the kitchen.

Rosemary hung in the air. It smelled like Thanksgiving, reminding me of family. I remembered what my mom said on the trip. "He's the only family I've got left."

I could see the kitchen table from where I was sitting, and I watched as Uncle Butch put the chicken in a pan. He yanked its legs apart and spread them wide while jamming and stuffing the small cavity with over-large hands. Then he tied the legs together with roasting string.

After he stuffed the chicken he went on to the porch, which was fine by me. He was the darkness that kept us down all day. He wore the darkness like my mother had at times, the times she felt lonely, although I was in the room with her.

At dinner, Wendy set the table while I got the milk. Aunt Lori followed us to the porch with the roasted chicken and put it on the table, then walked to the couch to pick up the newspapers that had collected there.

We heard a sound, like a baby crying. Aunt Lori went to the door to investigate.

"Oh my gosh, what's that on the step?" she asked.

With noses pressed to the screen, we could make out a closed picnic basket on the front step, bound in twine. Aunt Lori opened the door and picked it up. She raised the lid, and Oreo poked his head out and meowed.

"Well, would you look at that? I wonder where this came from." She unfolded a handwritten note. It read, "Thank you."

"Oreo!" I took the basket from her and two green eyes peered out at me. "This is the best surprise ever!"

"Can we keep him?" Paige asked.

Uncle Butch harrumphed. Everything was quiet for what seemed like eternity. "If that cat messes up in here, out he goes."

I got a shoebox from Aunt Lori and put torn newspaper inside of it for a makeshift litter box. Then we let Oreo wander around to get used to his new surroundings while we ate dinner. The whole time we were eating, I was trying to figure out who had delivered the basket, but I knew in my heart that it was someone on behalf of Mrs. Weaver.

Cleanup was fast so we could get back to Oreo.

"Who wants cake and ice cream?" Aunt Lori asked.

"I do," the three of us echoed. Oreo would have to wait.

Everyone had cake and ice cream, except for Uncle Butch, who was happy with his beer.

He looked up from the newspaper. "What are you doing, young lady?" His question was directed at Paige. We looked up from our cake and ice cream, confused. "What do you call this?" He pointed to her glass of milk. He waited for an answer, but Paige just gaped at him, frozen. "How many times have I told you to finish your milk? It's a sin to waste when children in other countries are starving to death."

"I don't want the milk. I want cake and ice cream. Besides, it's warm." Paige said.

I didn't know if she was stubborn or stupid. I held my breath.

"I don't care if it's warm, finish your milk."

"Why?"

"Because, I'm the adult and you are the child, and you do what I say."

"I won't drink it."

"You will drink it, or you won't eat your cake and ice cream."
No one moved. The Stare-Down began.

Paige picked up her fork and took a bite of her cake. She was a weird little nut to crack. I didn't know what would come next.

He put the newspaper down and shook his head in disbelief. He raised his bear claw as if to strike, but Paige remained silent. Then he picked up the glass of milk and poured it over her head. She had liquid white hair dripping down her face. Calmly, she wiped her face with her napkin and took another bite of cake. She spoke volumes with her silence. She became a princess wearing a crown of milk, and in my mind, I bowed down to her then.

"That's it." He grabbed her by the arm, pulled her up from the table, and forced her to our bedroom. "Stay in there until I tell you that you can come out."

On his way through the kitchen he grabbed another beer from the refrigerator and stormed back onto the porch.

"I'm going to drive Chris over to the house so she can call her mom," he said, after a few minutes.

I looked at the clock. It was a little after six.

"Do you think that's a good idea?" Aunt Lori looked at him, then at his beer.

His gaze seemed to burn through her. He challenged her with his posture, his eyes. "Why not?"

She lowered her eyes from him. Then turned away and started cleaning the plates, scraping them into a brown paper grocery bag that served as the trash.

"Can I go?" Wendy looked hopeful.

"No, you're on restriction, young lady." He turned to me. "Let's go."

As bad as I wanted to talk to my mom, I was equally reluctant to go by myself with him to the house. He looked at me differently when he was drinking. I felt his eyes on my skin like steam in a shower. I climbed into the station wagon and looked back at Wendy. Wendy's eyes looked more haunted than my heart. We waved to each other until I couldn't see the cottage anymore. She blurred at the edges and the same feeling came over me as when I said good-bye to my mom.

MORE THAN THE rain loomed. My heart was burdened by what my future held. As if on cue, the bruised sky ruptured and angels everywhere began to cry. Fat droplets of rain flattened against the windshield and streamed down the glass, blurring the oncoming traffic momentarily between the rhythm of the wipers. Uncle Butch tight-knuckled the steering wheel as he caressed the edges of the wet, winding road. It felt like fifteen hours instead of fifteen minutes to get to the house. Lightning scarred the sky and a crack of thunder followed as we pulled into the driveway.

The house was dark and hot. Uncle Butch pushed past me and grabbed a beer out of the fridge. "It sure feels good to be home."

He popped open the can, chugged the beer, and slammed the empty can on the kitchen counter.

"Aw, that's good," he said and burped. He grabbed another one. "Maybe you'd like to go upstairs and take a long, hot bath before you call your mom. It's a luxury we don't have at the cottage."

I felt uncomfortable in his presence, especially when he was drinking. I learned how to count the beers Uncle Butch had each night, and tonight he was on number seven. There was a darkness that crawled up inside him with each beer.

"No thanks. I'm going to call my mom now," I said and picked up the receiver. I waited until he was out of the room before I dialed the number.

It took three long rings before I heard my mother.

"Hello?"

"Hi, Mom," I said.

"Hi, Chris. It's so good to hear your voice again. I sure do miss you."

"I miss you too." I took a deep breath. "Mom?"

"Yeah, honey." She sounded so tired.

"I was wondering." Another deep breath. "When can I come home?" The edge in my voice was clear.

"What is it, honey? Is everything okay?"

"Yeah, but . . ." How was I going to tell her I knew about the divorce? I eased into it. "Have you heard from Dad?"

She let out a long sigh. "Yeah, but it's complicated."

The sadness in her voice vibrated through the phone. It made me want to cry. I took a few more deep breaths to shake the feeling.

"I know, Mom. That's why I want to come home. I can help."

"Chris, you have to give me some more time."

I wanted to scream-yell-cry. I said nothing.

"Please, honey. Can you just give me a little more time until I start feeling better?"

There was a quiver in her voice. She was pleading so I gave in. We were just talking around the "D" word anyway. "Okay, Mom. I hope you feel better soon."

"Yeah, me too, sweetie."

"I guess I'll see you soon, huh?"

"Yes, honey. See you soon."

She asked me a bunch of questions about what I'd been up to and I answered, trying to show her what a good time I was having. I told her about my new friends, about swimming at the pool, going to Coney Island, going to the dances. She seemed glad I was having fun with my cousins, but I guess she saw through me and asked about Reds specifically.

"Is he your boyfriend?" Her voice held a spark of excitement.

I did everything in my power not to squeal like a little girl. "Yeah. He asked me to be his girlfriend and he gave me a bracelet he made himself!" I touched the bracelet as I continued to talk about him. I think she was happy that I was finally having fun and not worrying so much about her.

We talked for a long while. After I hung up, I went to the family room where Uncle Butch was. It was dark even though the lights were on. It smelled like cigarettes and dirty socks. The couch, which was against the middle of one wall faced the television set. Two chairs were on the other wall. An end table with a lamp on top of it was in between them. Lightning blazed, and my shadow jumped crazily on the wall.

Uncle Butch had unbuttoned his shirt and he was standing in the middle of the room. His shoes and socks were by the couch. The radio was on and the music was radiating through the room. He was swaying to the music.

The ceiling fan cut shadows through the light, making it hard for me to focus.

"Come here and dance with me," he said, holding his hand out to me.

"No thanks." I was uncomfortable. I turned to leave, but he grabbed my arm and pulled me toward him before I could get away.

"Oh, come on. Come here and dance with me." This time it was a command.

"No, please, I don't want to dance."

"I showed you how to dance, remember?" He pulled me to his chest. I struggled, but my fight just wasn't as strong as his. "Dance with me." His voice was stern.

"No thanks."

"Awe, come on. I saw you dancing with that Johnson boy. You're quite the little dancer." He had both my hands in his. "Just relax and follow my lead."

He put my right hand on his chest and I felt the beating of his heart.

Dancing with Reds was exciting, full of unspoken promises. I loved his attention. But now I was just scared.

Without warning, he stopped dancing and held me in a tight embrace. I tried to push away, but he had a pretty good grip around my waist.

I squirmed to get away from him, but he pushed me down onto the couch and was on top of me in one quick movement. His hands were vice grips around my wrists, and when I tried to pull away, the bracelet Reds made me tore apart and dropped to the floor.

Fear, shock, and rage swept through me. The weight of his body kept me from moving. He was no longer my uncle but a stranger. A Monster. How could he be doing this to me? Why was this happening?

He was kissing me, and I couldn't breathe. I moved my head back and forth, causing his stubble to rake fire across my cheeks and mouth, but he didn't stop kissing me. I balled up my fists and pumped them against his chest, trying to get him away from me. I felt like I was drowning, like on the first day of summer in the river.

He finally stopped kissing me.

Gasping, I sucked in a great amount of air. *Lord, help me.*

"No! Stop!" I yelled.

His large palm covered my mouth, and I bit as hard as I could. I tasted blood, but that didn't stop him.

I entered a dream state, a state where I was a little girl playing with my mother in the front yard. She was teaching me how to suck the nectar out of honeysuckle. The images spilled against the white burning walls and disappeared before I could picture my mother's face completely.

I threw up. The sound that issued forth came from deep within my throat, a primal scream of an animal. It cracked like thunder in my eardrums, shattering my thoughts.

I saw spinning shadows across my eyelids, turning the light from dark to bright, dark to bright. It was the twirling propeller of a helicopter taking me to the hospital.

But I woke up, and it wasn't the propeller of a helicopter but the ceiling fan spinning the light into shadows. I was lying on my back on the couch, unable to move. The music was still on and every beat, every note pulsed inside my hurt and broken body. Vomit clung to my hair and spattered the front of my shirt. Uncle Butch was standing beside me. His appearance seemed to have changed. His hair was wet and combed back into a ducktail.

He picked up a framed photograph from the table and examined it. He put it back down, and I looked at it too. It was a young Uncle Butch, holding a dance trophy. In the background there was a banner that read: Winter Dance Contest. He appeared happy in the photograph.

I imagined that he was transported back to that dance contest. He reached out, remembering a judge handing him a trophy. There was an arrogance to him.

Like a man in a dream, he caught the music on the downbeat, took a turn while spinning on the ball of his foot, and quickly brought the other over with a slide.

As he continued to dance, the movements became that of a teenage boy. He looked right through me as if I weren't there, cutting me out with razorblade eyes.

I shifted my gaze down at the floor and spotted my bracelet. It was the only thing I had of Reds, so I reached down and picked it up. I didn't know if it could be fixed, but I tucked it in my pocket anyway.

I stood up slowly on unsteady legs.

He noticed me then and stopped dancing. "Let's go."

He didn't even give me time to clean up.

When we got in the car to leave, he leaned toward me and spit-whispered into my ear. "This never happened." Then he moved his sausage finger across my neck, a cutting blade that would sever me if I said anything. His smile was like blood.

On the way back, the sky was full of swollen clouds and it started raining after a few minutes. We drove through a great bath of tears in the stuffy car. There was an uncomfortable silence between us. Uncle Butch's knuckles were white from squeezing the steering wheel so hard. He picked up his Lucky Strike from the ash tray and sucked on the end long and hard.

The red glow illuminated his face momentarily. It looked like it was molded from clay with clumsy hands. Deep shadows crawled into his wrinkles making him look old.

"You know, if your mother ever found out, it would just kill her." He shook his head, almost talking to himself. "It would just kill her." He looked at me intently, just stared at me, waiting for me to say something.

I was silent. I stared out my window, refusing to look at him.

"Without family, you're nobody, with nobody to love and nobody to love you back . . . And now that your father is out of the picture . . . You'd be all alone."

I already felt alone. And he was right about my mother. It *would* kill her. He was pushing me further into a jail cell and dangling the keys in front of me.

"And then what? Who would raise you then if that happened?"

I remained silent.

"Me, that's who."

Oh my God. Everything he was saying was right. I squeezed the door handle. What would happen if I just threw myself out of the car?

He put his bear claw on my shoulder. "Are you listening to me?"

Out of fear I nodded, but I still didn't look at him.

"This never happened. Got it?"

I was breathing but I didn't feel alive. I wanted to scream, but couldn't. It's as if my mouth filled with mud, absorbing the words. I couldn't make sense of the world.

"Got it?" he said, louder, more insistent.

"Yeah, got it," I said, hissing like the caged animal I was.

"Good," he said. But there was nothing good left in my life. Where was Lisa's God now? The one who never dealt more than you could handle.

BACK IN THE safety of Aunt Lori, I tucked the horror of what had happened to me into my heart of darkness.

She saw me and her eyes widened as she quickly escorted me into the kitchen to get a better look. "What happened to you, sweetie?" The radio was playing but there was no more music in my heart, no harmony that would make me feel better.

I opened my mouth but nothing came out.

"She must have a stomach virus," Uncle Butch said. "She got sick as soon as we pulled into the driveway. I guess the cake got the best of her."

It felt like sharp splintered glass had lodged in my heart. My silence was my shame.

Wendy handed me clean pajamas and underwear, and I changed in the bathroom. It hurt between my legs, and I could barely move. I remembered Reds caressing my thighs at the pool, but now they were turning purple. I tossed my underwear into the dirty clothes pile, blood stains and all. That's exactly where I felt I belonged.

I got back to the kitchen. Aunt Lori was waiting for me at the sink. The coldness trailed behind Uncle Butch like smoke as he left the room, a ghost in his wake. *This never happened.*

In my daydream state, I could feel the gentle hands of my aunt as she washed away the puke from my hair, felt her breasts against my back. Although the water was cold in the kitchen sink, it was soapy and cleansing. I felt the love and safety of her as she stroked her fingers through my wet hair. I pictured my mother washing my hair, soothing me. Loving me. Saving me from The Monster.

She turned the water off and handed me a dry towel to twist over my head. I looked into her "don't rock the boat, baby" eyes and knew she couldn't help me.

After I dried my hair, I went to bed. I didn't cry until I knew everyone was asleep. My teardrops told the story as they fell down my face and cotton candy clouds became sugarless in my new tissue paper world. The world where the boogey man lived in my own backyard.

CHAPTER TWELVE
DEAD FISH EYES

I KEPT MYSELF in the position I fell asleep in, which was with my knees pulled in tight to my chest. My mouth was dry and I couldn't swallow, like I had licked cement all night. The rain clouds had cleared and gave way to the rising sun. I looked over at my cousins on the bunk beds who were still sleeping.

I heard my uncle's voice, and a pain ran through my body.

"Good morning, sweetie. How's my beautiful wife today?" He hadn't shaken the frogs loose from his voice yet.

"Why are you in such a good mood?" Aunt Lori asked.

"No reason."

"You're up and dressed early this morning."

"I'm going fishing with Bob. I don't know when I'll be back."

"Okay. But first, I'll make you breakfast."

I heard the clicking of the gas stove as she lit a burner and then the scrape of an iron skillet being placed on it. Then I heard a tap, tap, and the crack of an eggshell. Bacon sizzled and filled the cottage with its smell.

The window was open and a warm breeze wrapped around my body. The sun crept through the lace curtains, creating jagged shadows in the room. I remained frozen for fear he might hear me if I moved. My heart pounded in my chest against my ribs, and I was burning between my legs.

I closed my eyes and I was stuck inside my darkness for what seemed like hours. I couldn't shake the image of his sweating face above mine. I remembered the red spider veins across his nose, the oil on his forehead, and the urgency in his eyes and how they looked right through me. I heard his voice blowing hot in my ear. *"Do you need me?"*

I don't know how long I had been in my nightmare when I heard the crank of his car engine. Then I heard the station wagon pull away from the cottage. Only then did I take a deep breath and stretch my legs out. I moved slowly because of the bruises on my thighs and the pain I felt bone deep within my body.

Wendy nudged me. "What's wrong? Why aren't you getting out of bed?"

I wanted to tell her that her daddy was a monster, but the words were stuck in my throat. I couldn't utter one single syllable. I thought of my grandfather and his throat cancer. How Mom said he couldn't express his feelings even though his mind was still clear. He was a prisoner in his own body. That's the way I felt.

The truth was muddy and dirty and sharp. It would cut my throat if I spoke.

I needed the pen my dad had given me. I needed red ink!

I studied Wendy's face as if I had just seen her for the first time, looking for *him* in her features, but she looked just like her mother. Paige, on the other hand, had her dad's dark brooding looks and I felt sorry for her then. "I'll get up in a minute."

After they left, I waited a few more minutes before I forced myself out of bed and to the breakfast table. I sat down at my usual spot across from Uncle Butch's seat. I could still feel his presence, could still smell his cigarette.

I looked at his empty plate. It was smeared with egg yolk and had a cigarette butt sticking up from the mess. Next to his plate was his "World's Best Dad" coffee mug. A drip of coffee was still on the rim.

"Live and Let Die" came on and I went to the radio and turned it up. I heard the words with new meaning and with every sharp note, every crashing of the symbols, anger ran through me. I thought of Uncle Butch sweating over me. I did not want to 'Live and let live" anymore. I no longer wanted to give in and cry. I was sing-yelling all the words, spinning and dancing to the song and when it was finished, my senses were scattered in a sharp chorus of pain.

I pounded the table and then quickly swept my hand across it where Uncle Butch had been, swiping the mug off the table. It went crashing to the floor and broke into tiny pieces.

"What did you do that for?" Wendy asked.

"I don't know." But I did know and I blurted out, "I'm mad. Really mad," before I could stop myself.

Paige was looking at me with her brows furrowed, listening with her ear cocked toward me. She was trying to figure me out I guess, but she didn't say anything.

"Why are you so mad? Is it because we're on restriction?" Wendy asked.

"No, just drop it, okay?" I whispered so Aunt Lori wouldn't hear, but she heard anyway.

She came into the room to see what had happened. She looked at me, then at the pieces of the mug on the floor.

"It was an accident," Wendy said. She nudged my knee under the table with hers. I wanted to hug her, but didn't.

But then Paige spoke up. "She's mad, Mama. *Really* mad."

Aunt Lori looked at me with questioning eyes. Could she see my pain? My guilt? "Oh, honey. I know." She put her hand on my shoulder. "I know you must be frustrated that you're stuck here so far away from your mother and your friends . . . stuck here in a new place. But it will get better, I promise."

How could she be so nice yet so clueless?

"It's not that." Say it. Scream it. Just tell her! Tell everyone!

"Are you upset that it's Father's Day? Do you miss your dad, sweetie?"

I was silent. I didn't even know it was Father's Day.

"I'm sorry about your parents getting a divorce. I know how awful you must feel . . . not knowing what's going to happen to your family," Aunt Lori said. She gave me The Sympathy Smile.

Oh great. She just made everything worse, if that were possible. I hated The Sympathy Smile.

That was the thing that pushed me to the edge. I was going to Rock The Boat. I was going to Tip The Boat Over!

The words formed deep in my throat. I opened my mouth to speak, but my words were stuck in my throat. I squeaked instead. An unrecognizable "Gaw" escaped.

"Are you okay?" Aunt Lori asked.

Oh God, oh God, oh God. Please give me my voice back.

Aunt Lori kept looking at me, waiting for an answer. She walked over to me and brushed my hair away from my face.

I nodded. Tears slipped down my cheeks.

"I know it's hard, honey, but everything will be okay. I promise."

She shouldn't make promises that she couldn't keep.

"Now, is anyone hurt?" Aunt Lori asked while bending down and picking up the bigger pieces.

We shook our heads. It was quiet and everything was still. She looked at each of us and when she was convinced no one was cut and bleeding, got the broom from the kitchen. I watched as she swept the little white lie into the dust pan and into the trash where it belonged.

"Where's Daddy?" Paige asked. The question got my stomach all twisted in a knot again.

"He went fishing, sweetie. He'll be back later," Aunt Lori said, returning to the kitchen with the broom in her hand.

Paige pushed her tongue out through the space of her two missing front teeth. "Momma, I feel a tooth coming in."

"Really?" Aunt Lori came back onto the porch. "Let me see." She bent over and examined Paige's front teeth. "Yep, you're getting your first adult tooth." She rubbed the top of Paige's head.

After breakfast, I took my plate to the kitchen sink where Aunt Lori was washing the dried eggs from the iron skillet.

"Chris?" she said.

"Hmm?" Still no voice. Had she seen me swipe the coffee mug off the table?

"How are you feeling this morning? You seemed pretty sick last night."

"Um . . ." Squeak, squeak. Nothing in my life was the way I thought it would be. Not my mother, or the aching loneliness that kept me from falling asleep at night, not even my so called vacation.

"Come with me. I want to talk to you alone for a minute."

"Okay." I followed her to our bedroom and she sat on my bed.

I heard Uncle Butch's voice in my head. *This never happened.* I wanted to scream but was too afraid.

She patted the space next to her and I sat down. She pushed my hair behind my ears, something my mom used to do too.

"Honey, I saw the blood on your underwear." Her eyes were burning through me, reaching for my heart. She sees my pain, hears my screams. "You should have told me."

"I wanted to." My voice escaped through gasping cries of relief. "I thought everyone would be mad at me, like I did something wrong. I was so afraid."

"You shouldn't be afraid that you started."

"Started what?" I asked through sobs, confused.

"Started your period. There's no shame in it. Every woman goes through it." Aunt Lori looked at me with a knowing smile and winked.

I hadn't had a period yet so I didn't know what to think. I panicked, and my voice left me as she kept talking.

"Has your mother talked to you about your menstrual cycle?"

I shook my head in defeat.

"Well, sweetie, it's when your body starts to change into a woman's . . . and that means you are able to have babies." She patted my knee. "Soon, you'll get boobs and you'll start to fill out and get some curves on that boney body of yours." She patted my knee like I was a little girl. I cringed.

"Why can't my mom come get me Aunt Lori?" I had the mother of all secrets squeezing my heart and sneaking up my throat, twisting around my vocal cords. I couldn't talk so I cried instead.

She sighed. "Honey, I'm sorry. I know that I shouldn't be the one to give you this talk; it should be your mom sitting here next to you. I know you're frustrated. But things will get better soon. I promise. I'm sure she can explain all of this to you better than I can. Your mom will be here in no time. Meanwhile, let's just make the best of things, okay?" She put her arm around my shoulder and squeezed me to her.

I nodded.

"We need to do something about your bloody underwear, though, sweetie. You can't go around bleeding all day. You stay right here. I'll be right back."

She left the bedroom and when she returned, she had something in her hands. She held up her right one first. "This is a pad. You put it in your underwear when you are on your period and it will catch the blood. It's pretty simple. You just peel off the backing, put it in your underwear, and wa-la, you're done."

Then she held up her left hand and produced a white cardboard tube with a string hanging from its end. "This is a bit trickier." She pointed to the end with the cotton protruding from it. "You put this end inside yourself, and then push the bottom half up and it releases the tampon inside, see?" She demonstrated by pushing the bottom half of the cardboard up and a tube of pressed cotton sprang lose from the thing. It rocketed in an arch across my knee with the string attached and landed on the bed next to me.

I examined the tampon and then the pad. "I'll use the pads," I said in order to make my aunt happy and to shut her up about the whole menstrual cycle thing.

Shut up, shut up, shut up.

I know she kept talking, but I disappeared into my mind.

She finally finished and hugged me. Her touch felt empty, but I still didn't want her to let me go.

"It'll be okay." Aunt Lori rocked me in her embrace. "I just had to give Wendy the same talk last summer."

Oh no. Wendy! I wondered then. Was I his first? His last?

Instantly I became afraid for Wendy. It hurt me to think that The Monster could have hurt her too. I leaned forward and groaned.

"What is it, honey?"

More groans.

"You sound like you're hurting."

I nodded.

"That's the cramps, sweetie. Menstrual cramps. They'll go away. Sometimes it helps to take a cold shower."

After she left the bedroom, I laid down on the bed and pulled my legs up tight to my chest. A few minutes later Oreo jumped up on the bed. He lay down next to me and started purring. That sound, the sound of happiness, comforted me. It softened all the sharp edges of life. It was my favorite sound in the whole world. Then he started making biscuits with his paws. That was what my mom called it when cats kneaded their front paws on something soft, but I knew that's what they did when they wanted to nurse.

I rubbed his head. "I know you want your mother. I want my mine too."

I cried softly so no one would hear me. My tears disappeared into his fur, but he didn't care. He was my only confidant.

Since I didn't sleep much the night before, I was dead tired. I listened to Oreo purring until I fell asleep.

After I got up, I went to the porch and found my cousins and aunt at the table, playing cards.

"Are you feeling better, honey?" Aunt Lori asked.

"A little," I lied.

I sat down to join them but as soon as I did, I heard Uncle Butch's car approaching. I immediately tensed up and my palms got sweaty.

A few seconds later he pulled the car up in front of the porch and parked. I watched through the screen to see what would happen next.

Uncle Butch and Bob got out of the station wagon and stretched. Then Uncle Butch pulled a white bucket out from the trunk while Bob removed his fishing pole.

"Your daddy sure is a good fisherman," Bob said.

"He's not my daddy," I said, but no one heard me.

"See you later, Butch," Bob said and then went into his cottage.

After Bob left, Uncle Butch reached inside the bucket. With a swoosh, he held up a stringer of fish. "I got dinner."

"Daddy's home and he has some fish," Paige called out to her mother excitedly.

Aunt Lori walked over to the door. "Well, I'll be." She had a genuine smile. I wanted to run to her and hide from The Monster, but I was frozen.

I looked at the fish, each one strung from gill to mouth on the thin rope, spots of blood on their bodies and running from their mouths. Even though there was a screen between us, I could still see their dead hopeless eyes.

"You'll have to clean them. I don't want to have anything to do with all that mess." A strand of Aunt Lori's blond hair fell across the side of her face and she brushed it off.

"It's just a little blood and guts. It won't kill you." He walked to the picnic table in the muddy yard and set the fish down. Aunt Lori sighed and went into the kitchen while I continued watching Uncle Butch.

He walked back over to the car and got out his tackle box, then went back over to the fish. He pulled out a filet knife. It gleamed in the sunlight. "Come here, girls. I'll show you how to clean a fish." I remained a chameleon, blending into the background to avoid The Monster that had replaced Uncle Butch.

The screen door banged shut as Paige ran to her dad. He put the knife down and hugged her. Wendy stayed on the porch with me.

He looked at us. "Wendy, bring me some newspaper would you, honey?"

"Are you coming?" Wendy asked me.

I shook my head.

"I'm sorry you don't feel good," she said. She smiled a genuine smile. Not the fake Sympathy Smile Aunt Lori gave me. "Sorry about your dad too." She said so much without saying anything at all. She seemed smarter than a thirteen year old. Smarter than both Aunt Lori and Uncle Butch.

At that moment, I realized that I loved her like a sister. "Thanks."

Wendy reluctantly grabbed a pile of old newspaper and went to her dad.

"You don't want to learn how to gut a fish, Chris?" He gave me The Stare Down. His eyes searched mine, like he was waiting for me to say something. Something about last night. It took me a few seconds, and then I realized that it wasn't just a look, but a challenge. Would I say anything about last night?

"No. I don't want to see any blood or guts."

"Okay. But you don't know what you're missing," Uncle Butch said.

Wendy and Paige shrugged and turned their attention to Uncle Butch, who reached into the bucket and removed a fish from the stringer. I went to our bedroom to watch from a safer distance.

I knew what was in store for those dead fish. With one push, Uncle Butch inserted the filet knife into the belly and wiggled it up to the head. He took his thumbs and spread the fish wide, allowing for the guts to spill out from the body.

Aunt Lori came into the bedroom while I was looking out the window. She put her arm on my shoulder. "Honey, where are your cousins?"

"They're outside helping Uncle Butch clean the fish."

"What?" She looked out the window just as Uncle Butch handed the knife to Wendy. Then Wendy plunged the knife into the belly of a limp fish. She forced the knife up toward the head, struggling to keep hold of the fish and the knife.

After a minute of struggling, she lost her grip and the knife landed point down just inches from her foot. Uncle Butch plucked the knife from the ground and held it up in front of him.

"It's okay. That was good for your first try." He took the fish from her and placed the blade into the cut she had started. "Let me show you the proper way to do it." He plunged the knife deep into its belly and forced his way up to the head.

"I swear that man doesn't have a lick of sense sometimes." She left and I looked back out the window to watch.

"I don't want those girls around that knife! You hear me?" Aunt Lori said from the porch.

"They're not going to get hurt," Uncle Butch said.

"I just watched as Wendy almost lost a toe!"

"You're exaggerating. Besides, you treat them like they're babies."

"And you treat them like they're adults, and they're not." She yelled louder than I have ever heard her. It made me nervous because I had never heard her raise her voice to him before. Everybody stopped talking.

He looked at her for a long while, then turned quickly and plunged the knife into the picnic table. The handle wobbled and then steadied itself.

I thought about Uncle Butch and the fish all day, but I didn't have to see him again until dinner. Aunt Lori had fried the fish in beer batter and the whole house smelled like fish and grease. Every time I looked at my plate, I saw those dead fish eyes staring up at me. I ate my hushpuppies and corn, but pushed the fish around on my plate. I just couldn't bring myself to put the fish into my mouth.

"May I be excused?" The fish smell stuck to me like sweat, and I felt the need to shower.

"What is it, honey? Are you still feeling bad?" Aunt Lori asked.

"Yeah." I rubbed my abdomen. "Cramps."

"Okay, sweetie, you're excused."

Uncle Butch was shoveling fish into his mouth. Then he put his fork down and looked up at me with his black eyes. "Chris, will you get me another beer while you're up?"

I didn't move.

"Honey, is everything okay?" Aunt Lori asked.

"No."

"What is it?" Aunt Lori asked.

I looked hard at Uncle Butch. He shifted uncomfortably in his chair. He was holding his breath, staring at me.

"What is it?" Aunt Lori asked again.

A riot was forming in my head and I couldn't think. I was going to tell!

But then I remembered what he said about my mother. About how the truth would kill my mother and me becoming an orphan. If I told, it would also hurt my aunt and cousins, spreading the pain even more, changing everyone's life forever. It just seemed like it would cause a huge ripple effect and we would all drown from the pain that The Monster had caused. Was that fair?

I lost my nerve. "Nothing."

In his victory of keeping me silent, he said again, "Chris, get me a beer."

Everyone stopped talking. Aunt Lori sized me up. She looked like she was trying to figure something out about me.

"I'll get the beer," Wendy said. She was becoming my protector.

"Thank you, sweetie," Uncle Butch said.

No one knew what I was feeling. The riot was now blinding me and I left, leaving everyone but Uncle Butch in a state of confusion.

I went to the bathroom to take a shower and to cool off. While in the shower, I clenched my hands into fists. My red painted fingernails looked like drops of blood against my skin.

I soaped up my body, starting with my face and working my way down my body. My face, my arms, my chest.

My thighs.

The thighs that Reds caressed in the pool. The thighs my uncle bruised. I felt so dirty. I scrubbed between my legs, over my thighs again. I repeated the action over and over again as if I could erase the feeling of their touch. Erase what happened. But as hard as I tried, no amount of soap could make me feel clean.

CHAPTER THIRTEEN
TRAPPED

SINCE WE WERE on restriction, the time passed slowly. By Tuesday, Aunt Lori felt sorry for us, so after breakfast she asked, "Wendy, do you guys want to go to the pool with us today? I promise I won't tell your father."

"Okay," Wendy said.

I wanted to go too, but then I thought about my bruised thighs. I did a good job of hiding them under my clothes, but I couldn't hide them in just a bathing suit. "No, it's okay. I don't want to go." I was a prisoner not only in the cottage, but in my own skin.

Wendy looked at me, puzzled. "Why? This is our chance to get out of the cottage."

"I know. I just don't want to go." I shrugged. "But you should go."

She thought about it, a little too long, then reluctantly said, "No, it's okay, I'll stay here with you."

"Suit yourselves," Aunt Lori said, disappearing into the master bedroom.

"Why don't you want to go?" Wendy asked.

I dreaded the question and didn't want to get into it. How was I going to explain my black and blue bruises? I shrugged and left it at that.

Wendy and I spent most of the day watching the antics of Oreo and chasing him around. We talked a lot but there was a cloud hanging over us. Like Wendy wanted to ask me something but couldn't. It became a big fat question mark that we both ignored.

A few hours later, Aunt Lori and Paige returned. After

Paige changed out of her wet bathing suit, she plopped down next to us on the couch in the living room.

"Are you and Mom going to the pool again tomorrow?" Wendy asked.

"I think so, why?"

"I want you to find out from Julie what's going on with the gang," Wendy said. We hadn't seen or talked to anyone since the dance on Friday before we were grounded.

"Julie will never talk to me," Paige said.

"I know, but I want you to give her a note. Can you do that for me?" Wendy asked.

"Why should I?"

"Paige? Will you do it for me if you won't do it for Wendy?" I asked. She seemed reluctant, so I used my secret weapon. "Please? I'll let you sleep with Oreo tonight."

"You will?" She didn't seem to believe me. "You promise?"

"Yes, I promise. Will you please try? That's all I ask." I put Oreo down and he went over to Paige and rubbed his head against her leg. She picked him up and kissed his tiny face.

"Okay." She cuddled the kitten a little too long and he squirmed to get down.

"Do you want to feed him?" I asked, to keep her from being disheartened.

We went into the kitchen and got the kitten food and scooped it into his bowl. Then I told her to wash his water bowl and fill it with fresh water. He had a healthy appetite for such a tiny kitten.

"You're going to be a fat cat if you keep eating like that, Oreo," I said.

Paige stroked him as he ate, but he didn't like it. He meowed at her.

"He just doesn't like when you touch him when he's eating," I said. "Wait until he's finished and then you can play with him."

Wendy and I got out a piece of paper and a pen and sat down at the kitchen table. We wrote a note to Julie. *What have you guys been doing? We've been on restriction since the dance.*

That sounded stupid so we started again. In her best handwriting, Wendy wrote,

Julie, we are on restriction, but we will be at the Fourth of July dance. Come by our cottage after work.

Wendy folded the note and gave it to Paige, but before she let go of it, she said sternly, "Don't let anyone see this. Give it to Julie tomorrow at the pool. Be sneaky. Slip it in under her towel or put it in her pool bag to make sure she gets it."

I looked at Wendy. We hadn't thought this through. "Okay, suppose Julie does get the note? Have you stopped to think that we may still be on restriction on the Fourth of July?"

"No," Wendy said.

"Why not?" I asked.

Wendy looked at me. "Well, for one thing, I've never missed a Fourth of July party at Shady Grove since I was born. For another thing, my dad loves the Fourth of July party because of the dance competition, which he and Mom have won seven years in a row. He's a legend at the party. Everyone comes to watch my parents dance, and he'll let us go because he loves an audience. Trust me."

"Do you think he'll let us go to the party this Friday night?"

"I don't know. I'll ask him tonight, if he's in a good mood, and see what he says."

"I hope so." I sank further into the couch cushions. Oreo jumped onto my lap and started purring.

Wendy played cards with Paige on the porch until Uncle Butch came home from work. As soon as he put his keys down on the table, Wendy went to the refrigerator and got him a beer.

"How was your day, Daddy?" She handed him the beer and he sat at the table and opened the beer first, then the newspaper.

I kept my distance from him as much as possible, careful not to look at him directly for fear he would use the now familiar Stare Down tactic to keep me quiet.

"Thanks, honey. Your daddy sure is tired." He took a swig of beer and then lit a cigarette. "What a terrible day."

Aunt Lori emerged from the kitchen and kissed him on the cheek. "Bad day?"

He put the newspaper down. "That lazy son of a—"

"Watch your language in front of the girls." Ironic. She wanted to protect me from Uncle Butch's bad words, but couldn't protect me from The Monster.

"Charlie took an order without checking to see if we had the supplies in, and told the customer that we could install her kitchen cabinets next week, and now I have to call her and explain . . ." He got up from the table, grabbed his beer, and took it with him as he left the cottage in a huff. The door slammed behind him.

Aunt Lori sighed heavily.

"Is Daddy okay?" Paige asked.

"He's just a little stressed about work, that's all. Everything's okay. Go back to playing. Dinner will be ready in an hour."

They continued playing cards.

He came back a half hour later and didn't seem any better. He sat in the chair that seemed to have lost all its stuffing.

I didn't dare move for fear I would cause unwanted attention. I was getting good at becoming a chameleon, blending into the background. I avoided drawing attention to myself as much as possible.

At dinner, he sat across from me. I didn't need to look up from my plate to know he was looking at me. I felt hot under his stare.

After dinner, Paige complained of a headache.

"Come with me and let me see if you have a fever." Paige, Wendy and I followed Aunt Lori to the kitchen. She put her cheek on Paige's forehead. "You feel warm." She reached into the kitchen cabinet for the bottle of aspirin, and she shook one out from the bottle into her palm and held it out for Paige. "Here, take this." She grabbed a glass and filled it with water and handed it to Paige.

"I don't want to," Paige said. "I can't swallow it."

"You have to, just try."

Paige put the aspirin in her mouth, took a large sip of water, and threw her head back. Then she threw up the pill into the sink.

"Oh, Paige." Aunt Lori shook another aspirin out into her palm and told Paige to hold her head back. Then she threw the aspirin way back into Paige's mouth and gave her a sip of water. Again, the pill choked her, and she spit it into the sink.

"I don't know what I'm going to do with you. You need the aspirin to lower your fever," Aunt Lori said, frustrated.

Uncle Butch came into the kitchen. "What's going on in here?"

"I can't get the aspirin down Paige's throat."

"Here, give it to me." He forced Paige's head back, stuffed the aspirin down the back of her throat, gave her a sip of water, then pinched her nose closed with his big sausage fingers and covered her mouth with his palm. Paige squirmed.

"She can't breathe, stop it." Aunt Lori tried to pull his hand from Paige, but it was no use. He was stronger and more determined.

"No. You need to be the one in control. Let 'em know who's boss," Uncle Butch said.

Paige started shaking her head back and forth and the more she shook, the stronger his grasp was on her. Her face was turning blue.

I remembered that night. The night I couldn't breathe.

I heard a whisper in my ear. *Be Brave.* "Stop!" I didn't really have a plan, I just needed to save my cousin.

Uncle Butch cut me a look. He gave me The Stare Down.

He released his grip from around Paige's nose.

Finally, Paige breathed. She opened her mouth, sucked in a huge amount of air, and coughed violently.

"My mom dissolves the aspirin in some sugar water and—"

Aunt Lori seemed relieved. "Well, that's a great idea." She quickly dropped an aspirin into a glass, added enough water to cover the bottom and poured in a little sugar. Then she took a spoon and crushed the pill in the sugar water. She stirred and handed the glass to Paige.

Paige swallowed the mixture and placed the glass on the counter and glared at her father. Aunt Lori tucked her into a hug. The four of us kept our eyes on Uncle Butch.

"I was just doing what my father did to me when I couldn't swallow a little pill! That's the way it's always been done!" Uncle Butch's face reddened and he turned to leave.

"Well, it's time for a change," I said, but he didn't hear me because he was already gone.

Aunt Lori smiled and winked at me. I felt a little surge of victory.

CHAPTER FOURTEEN
PICTURE PERFECT

THE NEXT DAY, Wendy whined quietly to her mother, "Mom, I'm so bored."

"Why don't you read a book?" Aunt Lori said.

"Mom, it's summer!" Wendy seemed offended by the suggestion.

I was entertaining myself by watching Oreo trying to catch a fly. I thought reading a book was a good idea. I loved to read.

"It's not against the law to read over the summer, you know," Aunt Lori encouraged. "Go look in the trunk in my bedroom. I think there are some books in there. They might be old, but sometimes the oldies are the goodies."

"I don't want to read," Wendy said, pouting.

"Well, there are probably some games in there, too. Just go have a look."

"Okay," Wendy surrendered. "Come on, Chris."

I scooped up Oreo and took him with us. The trunk was at the foot of bed, and we flipped the latches and opened the top. We rummaged through paperback books and a few games that looked old and unfamiliar, and then we found some larger hardback books. I pulled one of those out. "What's this?"

"Let me see." Wendy took it from me. "Hey, this is my mom's old yearbook."

She opened it up. "Let's look at it." She jumped up on the bed. "Come on." She patted the bed, motioning me to sit next to her.

"Okay. I bet my mom's in here too," I said as I got on the bed, Oreo close behind me. We lay on our stomachs next to each other so we could both see the pages. Oreo found some fringe on the throw pillows to entertain himself. I loved him, and I whispered my secrets nightly into his furry ear. He kept me from the shadow world for the most part. I couldn't wait for Mom to meet him. Lisa was going to go crazy when I returned back home with a kitten.

Wendy flipped to the section where the mug shots were lined up in rows alphabetically by last name and by class. We looked through the freshman class first, and then sophomore, and then we found my mom in the junior year section.

"There she is." Wendy pointed.

I bit my lip, trying to keep from laughing until Wendy giggled.

"Look at that hair!" It was up in a beehive.

Then we flipped through the sophomore class, looking for Aunt Lori. My eyes spotted her long blond hair first, and I pointed to her photo.

"There she is. Gosh, she's so pretty."

"Thank you sweetie," Aunt Lori said from the doorway. I didn't know she was there.

"I think you're pretty too, Mom," Wendy said.

Aunt Lori laughed and went back to cleaning.

"Hey, isn't that your dad?" I pointed to the opposite page.

Wendy looked at the photo. "Yep, that's him."

His hair was too much to ignore, and I had to say something. After all, one small stab at him was a drop in the bucket compared to what he did to me.

"What did he use, motor oil?" I giggled.

His hair was jet black and slicked back on his head, except for the one thick curl that hung down on his forehead. You could see where the teeth of the comb had left their impression.

"That's the way they wore it in the fifties," Wendy said.

I looked at the next page. "Hey, is that him too?" Uncle Butch was standing on a platform in the middle of a gym, but it didn't look like a sporting event.

Wendy slid the book over to where she could see the page better. "Yeah. What does he have in his hand?"

"It's a trophy. What's it for?" I asked.

"I know what it is," Wendy said. "It's a dance trophy. Remember, he said he was a dance champion or something."

I looked closer at the picture. There in the background was a banner that read: Winter Dance Competition. Then it hit me. That was the same photograph my uncle was looking at in Mount Adams! I shivered and looked away from the yearbook. I squeezed my eyes closed, trying to block the memories of that night. But it was no good. I couldn't shake the queasy feeling that had come over me. The urgency in Uncle Butch's eyes and his red spider webbed nose appeared so clearly on the back of my eyelids that I gasped. I kept reminding myself that every day I survived was one day closer to my mom.

"Are you okay?"

No, I wasn't okay and I wished everyone would just stop asking me. I wanted my mom, but I knew that was unlikely. So I did what I did most days, and I pushed the thought out of my head. I tried to act normal.

"Yeah. Just peachy."

I remembered that my mother also had high school accomplishments. "Hey, let's find my mom in the sports section." If I couldn't be with her, at least I could look at her photos to feel close to her.

"Okay." Wendy flipped to the section.

There she was, beautiful and young, and the depths of the photo captured my mother's smile, which was unmistakable and unique. The smile she had before my dad left. It made me homesick immediately.

"Hey." Wendy pointed to another picture of her on the opposite page. "Isn't that her, too?" She had found what I had hoped to find.

"Sure is. She was a runner," I said with great pride. The photo was glorious. My mother was breaking the finish ribbon; her head thrown back with chest pushed forward to claim first place. She was wearing her track and field uniform.

"That's so cool!" Wendy said.

"Yeah," I added, but turned the page because I didn't want to start feeling the pain of being away from her.

We flipped through the yearbook until we got to the last page. It turned out to be a dedication page. We spent a longer time looking at this page because it was a mystery. There were two photographs on it, but one was scratched out.

"Who's that?" Wendy asked, fingering the photo that had become a scribble of black ink. Whoever owned the pen that did the scratching was full of rage.

"I don't know, but someone sure didn't like her," I said.

Wendy read aloud *This yearbook is dedicated to the memory of Charles Weaver, and to his generous wife Mary, without whom the publication of this yearbook would not have been possible.*

I remembered the name "Weaver" painted on Mrs. Weaver's weathered mailbox. "Is that Crazy Mary?"

"I can't tell, it's all scratched out." Wendy looked closer, trying to distinguish a face.

"I know who would know." I jumped up with the book in my hand, scaring Oreo. "Your mom can tell us." We raced each other to the kitchen where Aunt Lori was sitting at the table playing solitaire. Wendy grabbed the book from me and threw it down on the table, open to the last page.

"Mom, is that Crazy Mary?"

Aunt Lori took the book and looked closer at the photo. "Well, I suppose it is. You're father scratched out her photo."

"I knew it," I said under my breath.

"Oh my gosh, this brings back memories." Aunt Lori flipped through the yearbook and found one of the pages that we had been looking at, the one with Uncle Butch receiving the dance trophy. "Well, there he is in all his glory. I believe this might have been your father's finest moment. He was the dance champion that year. No one in the school could come close to his ability."

"Mom, why did Dad scratch out her photo?"

"I'm getting to it, honey. You see, at the end of every school year we had a big, and I mean, big dance contest in the spring. Your father was a sure win since he won the winter contest. Every girl in school wanted to go with him to the dance. But not just for the glory. There was a two hundred dollar prize to be won—a contribution from the Weavers. Anyhow, your father was disqualified."

"Why?" Wendy asked

"Skipping school. He was caught skipping school by Mrs. Weaver, or Crazy Mary, as you guys like to call her. I remember it like yesterday. It was quite a scene. She marched him into the principal's office, mad as a hornet. She was banging her fist on the desk, demanding that the principal call the police."

"Did he rob her or destroy something on her property?" Wendy asked.

"Not to my knowledge. I still don't know what she was so infuriated about. Your father never told anyone. He just said, 'That old bat is crazy.' I guess that's how she got her nickname.

"Anyhow, plenty of girls were mad that your father wouldn't be dancing. I wasn't too happy either. We had started going out that year, and I was expecting to be his date. I would've won half of the prize money. Anyway, the principal said that he preferred to handle the matter within the school, and he suspended your dad. As the rules go, if you are suspended, you can't participate in any school-related activities. Oh, you should have heard your father throw a fit. I believe by that time the whole school was trying to get a peek at what was happening in that office. Mrs. Weaver was not too pleased. But I guess she accepted it, because she turned tail and stomped out of the building."

"So that's why dad hates her," Wendy said.

"I guess it is," Aunt Lori said and proceeded to flip through the pages.

"Lori, what are you girls doing in there? Send someone out with another beer would you?" Uncle Butch called from outside where he was talking to Bob. They were sitting at the picnic table.

"You take this and put it back where you found it." Aunt Lori handed Wendy the yearbook and resumed with her cards.

She came back with a game I had never played before, Mystery Date. We spent half the night trying to figure out the rules, but they were just as confusing as the ones in real life.

CHAPTER FIFTEEN
SCREENED IN

WE WERE ON the porch playing with Oreo when Julie showed up.

"Hi, guys. Got your note." She was wearing her red one piece bathing suit with a whistle around her neck and a towel over her shoulder.

I walked over to the screen where she was. Wendy followed me.

"Hi, Julie."

"Heard you guys were in jail, had to come by and see for myself." She was actually gloating. Seeing Julie out there with her freedom and her beauty made me ache to be like her, but I knew now that I never would be.

I envied her long-boned confidence. She was all curves and I was all angles and sharp edges. I would never have the wide-eyed innocence I had when I arrived. I had finally seen myself through the black eyes of Uncle Butch and I knew I came from a hard-boiled madness.

"Yeah, we shouldn't have left the dance early without telling my parents," Wendy said.

"How long are you guys locked up?"

"Don't know," I said, looking out of the screen that separated us. I had Oreo in my hands.

"What's that?"

"It's my kitten, Oreo."

"How cute," Julie said, moving away from the screen that served as the bars of our jail and sitting on top of the picnic table. A flash of light sparkled in my eye. Next to her was a patch of dried blood speckled with fish scales shinning like diamonds in the sunlight. It was Uncle Butch's fishy killing ground.

"Where's everyone else?" Wendy asked.

"Freckles' dad sent him to military school. He's training to become a marine or something like that. His dad really knocked him around. He had a black eye when he left."

"That's too bad," Wendy said.

With Freckles gone and us being on restriction, we didn't have the chance to drink, or smoke, or get into any more trouble, which was fine by me. I was tired of being in trouble, tired of being grown up.

"What about the others?" I asked, trying not to show too much enthusiasm.

"You mean Reds, don't you—you sly fox. And you want to know where Owl is. Right, Wendy?"

"Yeah," we echoed.

"I'll let them know where you are."

Uncle Butch pulled up in front of the cottage. I didn't know it was so late.

He got out of the car and walked over to Julie at the picnic table.

She stood up and stretched.

"Well, hello, Julie. It's been a while since you've been over here. This is a nice surprise."

"Hi, Mr. Morgan. How are you?"

"I'm better now. I didn't know a pretty girl was in my front yard. I would have come home sooner."

"Thanks, Mr. Morgan." I hated when her voice got all sugary. She loved attention and loved flirting, but she was flirting with the wrong person and I had to let her know. I didn't want her on my conscious too.

"I didn't know you were a life guard."

"Yeah." She fiddled with the whistle hanging around her neck. "I work at the pool here at camp. It's a good job. Plus I get to work on my tan."

Uncle Butch couldn't stop looking at her whistle.

God. How much longer could I watch this?

"I see you at the dances."

"I see you too. You and Mrs. Morgan are really good dancers."

"Thanks. Save me a dance, next time. I'll show you some moves."

I had to stop this. But before I could speak, Wendy spoke up first.

"That reminds me, Dad. Can we go to the dance tomorrow?" Her voice was louder than it needed to be, but it did the trick. It seemed to break the spell he seemed to be under. Had she felt the same uncomfortable feeling I had?

He hesitantly peeled his eyes from Julie's *whistle* and looked over at us.

"Nope."

"How about the Fourth of July. Can we go to that dance?" Wendy asked.

He thought about it for a moment. "I suppose so, if you promise to be good. I want to be able to see you two young ladies the entire time. Got it?"

"Yeah, we promise," Wendy said. Although I was defeated about Friday, at least we had the Fourth of July to look forward to.

"Well, when you guys get sprung, come over to the pool. I'll be life-guarding," Julie said. "Bye, Mr. Morgan."

"Bye, Julie. See you around."

I hope not. For being such a Monster, he sure was good at blending in and acting normal.

FRIDAY AFTERNOON, WHILE we were scarfing down a peanut butter and jelly sandwich, Reds and Owl showed up outside the porch.

"Hey, Chris," Reds said. "Good to see you. I was wondering where you've been. Did you hear about Freckles? He's in military school."

"Yeah, I heard."

"How long are you on restriction?" Reds asked. "Do you think you'll be at the dance tomorrow?"

I thought I missed Reds, but now as I looked at him, I was kind of afraid to be around him. I was glad for the company of Wendy, because I didn't know how I would feel if it was just the two of us.

"I doubt it. My uncle is still mad at us for disappearing at the last dance."

"The bicentennial celebration is coming up soon. Do you think you guys will be off restriction by then?" He put his hand up to the screen and I put mine up on top of it.

"I hope so," I said.

Then he put his lips to the screen. He looked funny, but innocent, too, so I kissed him back.

I tasted dust. The pressure of his lips on mine felt good. Safe. But ever since Mount Adams, I wasn't sure how to feel about Reds.

CHAPTER SIXTEEN
LIFE LINE

WHEN SATURDAY ARRIVED, I dreaded getting up in the morning. I was frightened about going to the house in Mount Adams, but I desperately wanted to talk to my mom.

As soon as it reached noon, Uncle Butch sat down at the table where we were having lunch. I kept my gaze down at my bowl of tomato soup. I avoided eye contact with him as much as I could. Today was no exception.

"Time to call your mom," Uncle Butch said. It was as if he was planning this moment all week. He even sounded happy about it.

I held onto the table half-expecting that I would drift off the porch. "Can Wendy come with me?" I asked with deepening uneasiness.

"I don't see why not," Aunt Lori said.

"I don't think that's a good idea," Uncle Butch said. His very presence made me tremble. "She's still on restriction. Also, I have to stop by the office and I don't need them running around in there." His voice was firm. I could see that Aunt Lori was reluctant to argue with him and would rather stay out of his way.

"Then I'm not going."

Uncle Butch cut me a malignant look.

I ignored him. I would rather pour pickle juice into my eyes than go to the house with him alone.

Aunt Lori walked over to me as soon as the words left my mouth. She knelt beside me and combed my hair back with her fingers. "What's the matter, honey?" she whispered.

The sheer act made me feel so comforted I could have cried. I wanted to cry, but I was too afraid. *This never happened* echoed in my head. I couldn't help it. I grabbed Aunt Lori and hugged her, burying my face deep in her neck.

"What's this? What's this all about? Don't you want to talk to your mother?" Aunt Lori asked.

How could I tell her? My uncle raped me, your husband. And what do I say to Wendy and Paige? Oh, by the way, your daddy is A Monster.

Aunt Lori looked directly into my eyes. "I'm sure she misses you terribly, and if she doesn't hear from you today, she might even come up here and get you." She laughed nervously.

"Please Daddy, can I come with you?" Wendy pleaded. "I won't get in the way."

He compromised. "No, but if you two young ladies promise to be good the rest of the weekend, I will lift the restriction." Wendy seemed happy with that and stopped pleading.

I had only just begun. "Please, Aunt Lori. Can Wendy come with me?"

Aunt Lori's voice caught, as if she was about to say something. Ask something. She was picking through the rubble, trying to figure things out.

"Yes. That's a great idea. I need some things at the house and Wendy can help get them." I don't know if she was figuring anything out or not, but I was thankful and let out my breath. I think this was the first time she verbally disagreed with Uncle Butch.

"Yay!" Wendy said.

Uncle Butch started to say something, but he hesitated like people did when they sense something was different.

I sat in the back and stared out the window, but I could feel his eyes on me. The car stopped, and Wendy went inside the house immediately. Uncle Butch got out of the car and stretched his legs. I was the last one out.

He threw his cigarette on the ground and snubbed it out with his shoe. Then he went into the house, leaving me standing alone in the gravel driveway. The tiny rocks threatened to push up through my flip flops as I walked toward the door.

I wasn't in any hurry to enter the house of horrors again, but I did want to call my mom, so I climbed the steps with cement shoes and entered the house. Wendy was already in the family room with the TV on.

Uncle Butch was standing in front of the refrigerator with the door open, most likely searching for a beer.

I walked to the phone hanging on the kitchen wall and picked up the receiver. I heard the first ring. "Come on, pick up," I said under my breath.

My feet were burning holes through the floor. I stretched all the coil out of the phone line and it was just enough to allow me to walk around the corner into the dining room. I felt like I was on a leash and he was my master. I leaned against the wall, hoping it would hold me up.

My mom finally answered on the third ring.

"Hello?"

"Mom?"

"Yeah, honey. It's good to hear from you."

"Mom, listen, you have to come and get me right now!" I whispered and was hoping she could hear the urgency in my voice.

"You're going to have to speak up, I can't hear you. We must have a bad connection."

"You need to pick me up. Now!" I whispered—yelled so Uncle Butch wouldn't hear me.

"Honey, what is it? What's wrong?"

"It's Uncle Butch. He . . ."

Uncle Butch was on me in one quick move, like . . . that night. He was standing right beside me running his sausage finger across my neck.

"What is it? You sound upset."

"Don't," he spit-whispered in my ear. He smelled like cigarettes and bologna. My ear was wet and I wiped his spit away.

"Nothing, Mom. I miss you is all."

"I know. And it won't be long now, I promise."

"Okay, Mom." I hoped she didn't hear the disappointment in my voice.

"Are you having fun? Are you getting along with your cousins?"

"Yeah. Getting along great." I couldn't help the sarcasm.

"Good. Tell everyone hello for me and I'll see you real soon."

"Okay. I love you," I said as I hung up the phone. I was disconnected from my mother, disconnected from the rest of the world.

Uncle Butch winked. "That's my girl."

He said it like it was a pat on the head. I felt the collar tighten around my neck, felt him pulling on the leash.

But I pulled back. "I'm not your girl!"

"You better watch yourself. Maybe I should take you down a notch."

"You do what *you* have to do, and I will do what *I* have to do." I turned away from him and called into the family room. "Wendy, it's time to go."

CHAPTER SEVENTEEN
THE PLOT THICKENS

THE NEXT MORNING the whole cottage was disrupted by the sound of Uncle Butch's yelling. "Wendy! Get in here and get this damn cat out of here!"

"What's wrong, Daddy?" Wendy jumped up and ran to her father's call. I followed close behind, concerned for Oreo.

"That stupid cat pissed all over my work clothes!"

"Calm down, Butch. You don't have to go to work until tomorrow. I'll have them cleaned for you by then."

"I'm sorry, Daddy. He's still a kitten. He doesn't know any better yet." Wendy picked up Oreo and handed him to me.

I took him in my arms immediately and carried him from the master bedroom to our bedroom as Uncle Butch continued to bluster.

"If that stupid animal can't learn to use a litter box, I will show him the door with the toe of my boot."

"You will do no such thing," Aunt Lori said. "He's still little. He'll learn. And don't scare the girls like that. They love that kitten."

"You just watch me!" Uncle Butch said as he stumbled around the bedroom. "I'll drown him in the river myself if I have to."

We were huddled around Oreo on my bed, but I could still hear Uncle Butch mumbling from the other room. I was scared for many different reasons. I had become a different, darker person and even entertained ways of getting back at him, The Monster, and today was no exception. Uncle Butch had shown me the meanness I was born into. I was meaner than a snake when the idea hit me, the whisper of venom coursing through my veins.

Oh yeah, I could be dangerous. I would show him just how dangerous I could be. I wanted to show him how it felt to be trapped by a snake.

I asked Paige to go feed Oreo for me because I wanted to share it with Wendy in private.

"Wendy?"

"Yeah?"

"I was thinking. Maybe there is a way for us to get back at him."

She looked interested. "How?"

"We're off restriction tomorrow, right?"

"Yeah," she said.

"Good, because it's going to involve the gang."

"What's the plan?"

"Well, you said it yourself. The thing he hates most. Snakes," I said. I felt devilish.

The next morning was the first day of our freedom. Since it was Monday, I stayed in bed until I heard Uncle Butch leave for work. After we got dressed and ate breakfast, Wendy and I walked to the river to meet up with the gang.

"It's so good to be out of that cottage," I said.

"I know. I was going stir crazy," Wendy said. "Plus, we get to see our friends again."

I could tell by the way she was skipping around that she was excited. But I also knew that going to the river was pushing the limits with Uncle Butch. He would punish us again in a heartbeat if he found out, and this time it wouldn't be just restriction. I felt queasy thinking about it, but the idea of getting my uncle back propelled me further on my mission.

We stumbled down the trail, flinging back branches, ducking under the brush, and tripping over twisted roots until we reached the opening. Above us, the sun struggled through the canopy of leaves. Long fingers of warmth trickled down around us.

I saw Julie first. The sun was streaking through the trees, making the highlights in her hair seem more golden, her tan darker. She was wearing a flowered sundress and sandals. Then I saw the boys off to the side huddled around in a semi-circle looking at something in Reds' hand. They didn't even notice us.

We walked up to Julie. The ground was covered with twigs and debris from high tide, and the muddy air was soft on my bare skin. The bottom half of the log in the clearing was still wet, and the dirt was damp but not muddy.

"What's going on over there?" Wendy asked, pointing to the guys.

"Reds found a praying mantis, so they all had to look at it. You know, birds of a feather and all," Julie said. She turned her attention to the boys. "Hey guys, look who it is. The prisoners have been released."

The sun was bouncing off the water and reflecting into our enclosure. Something about the water brought out the summer songs of the insects. The katydids, the frogs, and the crickets all seemed to be harmonizing. The birds had their own chorus. I soaked it all in.

Reds looked up, and then put the praying mantis on the branch of a tree. "Hey Chris. Hey Wendy. Good to see you guys."

The guys broke away from their bug circle and walked toward us.

"What's up?" Tommy asked.

Owl waved sheepishly, and Wendy waved back. His eyes seemed bigger than usual.

"How was it being locked up inside all day?" Reds asked.

"It feels so much better to be outside and to be by the river again," I said. Without Freckles, we were three pair instead of a full deck, and it felt weird not having him here with us. "Anyone know anything about Freckles since he's been gone?"

"No, nothing. Not since his dad sent him away," Julie said.

"With a black eye, too," Reds added.

"His dad was always a mean man," Tommy said.

"My dad can be mean sometimes too," Wendy said, surprising me. Had he hurt her too?

"Your dad? No way. He's the nicest man," Julie said. "Remember when he used to let us have sleepovers all the time?"

"He's not the nicest man," I said sharply. "Just because he thinks you're pretty and let you have sleepovers doesn't make him a nice man." I looked at Julie with an intensity I hoped she could feel.

Reds touched my arm and I quickly pulled away from him. "What's the matter?" Reds asked.

"Nothing." My voice went up in pitch. "I just don't think my uncle is the nicest man."

"Has he done something to you?" Reds asked.

I looked at him, frozen. Julie stared at me.

Speak. Tell. Do something! My throat was vibrating. Burning from the angry sharp words that were lodged there.

"Chris. What is it? Tell me," Reds said.

My mom told me that you should never air your dirty laundry in public. She also told me that the Morgans never showed weakness. Her wisdom got me through a whole lot of problems before. Maybe I should take her advice now.

"I don't know, just forget it." My moment of bravery slipped away.

"Well, he can be mean, especially when he drinks," Wendy said as if she was trying to come up with an excuse for me. It seemed like the question mark that had been following us around like a rain cloud was disintegrating. Her eyes grew moist.

I kicked off my flip flops and walked further into the shadows where the canopy of leaves blocked the sun entirely. I wanted to go deeper into the cavern as if plunging into the middle of it would hide my haunted soul. I sat on a fallen tree limb that was still damp. The mud seemed to be swallowing my feet, as if Mother Earth was pulling me into her.

There was a brief silence in which the distant echo of mockingbirds took me back to a place where I was just a girl sitting in the front yard and having a picnic with both my parents.

"At least he's interested in what you're doing, Julie said. "My parents couldn't care less about me. They're too busy with their own lives. I can get away with just about anything."

She craved attention, and got it too, but it was the attention of her mother that she wanted most. It was a shame that her mother was in the same room with her, yet so far away.

"I wish my parents were like that. Mine are too involved with my life," Tommy said. "My mom is a nurse and my father is the athletic director of the high school. I can't even piss without them knowing about it. Is your piss clear, Honey? Anything we should know about your piss, sweetie?" He sighed. "It's obnoxious, believe me."

"My parents are all right," Owl said.

"Mine too," Reds said.

"What about your parents, Chris?" Julie asked.

I wanted to tell them that my father was on an important business trip and would be back soon to be with me and he would bring me a present from some far off exotic place. I wanted to tell them that he was like the father on *The Brady Bunch* and that I had a whole house full of siblings. I would tell them that we all loved each other and were always there for one other. And I would tell them that when I hugged him, I would take in the smell of him. Like clean laundry hanging outside to dry.

And I would tell them how he liked to pick me up and put me on his shoulders when I was little. That he had a great laugh that started from his toes and rose up through his body. When he laughed it was so sincere and contagious that everyone around him couldn't help themselves but laugh too.

I would tell them that my mother was never sick and that she always took care of me, fussing over my hair and the clothes I wore. That she let me have sleepovers all the time and made me cookies for dessert. That she didn't have something called depression and had dropped me off at my cousins' cottage for the whole summer, but instead was taking me to Disney World on a family vacation with my father and my imaginary siblings.

That's what I would have told them. Instead I uttered what came to my mind first. "I wish I were adopted."

"Chris's parents are getting a divorce," Wendy said.

"I've never known anyone with divorced parents," Owl said quietly. I knew he didn't mean anything by it, he was simply stating a fact.

"Yeah, well, that's me," I said, my feet still imprisoned by the mud.

Reds walked over to me and sat down beside me. He put his hand around my shoulder and his hand trembled a little, and then settled. He didn't try to paw me like Uncle Butch, just comfort me.

Tommy walked over to Julie and wrapped his arms around her from behind. He was taller than her and she tucked her head under his chin. They made the perfect couple.

"Who wants to help me pull a prank on my uncle?" I asked.

"I do," Owl said, raising his hand.

"Well, of course *you* do, you pissed in a squirt gun for fun!" Tommy said.

"That sounds mean," Julie said. She smiled her evil smile. "I love it!"

"I'll help you Chris, but why?" Reds asked.

"Because he put us on restriction for no good reason," Wendy said.

I couldn't figure her out. Sometimes she seemed to be so clueless, but other times she seemed to want to help me out. Like now.

"And he threatened to drown my kitten," I said. "And I *know* he will do it too."

"Why does he want to kill your cat?" Julie asked.

"It doesn't matter. He threatened his life, that's the important thing. And I was thinking of a way to get back at him," I said. "You know, just to scare him a little."

"How?" Julie asked as if she had to approve of the plan first. I was getting real sick of her stupid questions.

"Reds, you'll catch the biggest snake you can find, not poisonous of course, and make sure I don't have to touch it," I said. "Then, you'll release the snake in the back door of our cottage right after my uncle starts his shower. It will crawl in there with him and scare the hell out of him."

"Yeah, he hates snakes. And when we see the look on his face, it will make up for all the time we've spent on restriction," Wendy said.

"I'll catch a snake for you, Chris. I like practical jokes and there are plenty of snakes around here by the water," Reds said.

The thought of snakes being so close around us made me shiver.

"Are you okay?" Reds asked.

"Yeah, I just don't like snakes. They scare me," I said.

"It might take a few days," Reds said.

"Okay," I said, excited. The plan was in motion. I felt close to Reds then. It gave us a common goal, bonding us in that moment.

"What do you want me to do?" Owl asked. He was so quiet I almost forgot he was there.

"You help Reds with the snake."

"Well, come on then. Let's go to my house and let the guys go hunting for snakes," Julie said.

"Okay," I said, standing up.

Reds stood too. He leaned in to me and kissed me softly on the lips. I didn't know how to feel about that. Our kiss through the screen felt safe, but now there was nothing between us. No barrier.

I tried to take a step forward, but my foot was stuck. I stumbled and almost lost my balance. I fell into Reds and he caught me. I laughed nervously.

"I got you. You're okay."

It felt good to be in his arms. For a moment I was just an innocent girl again and I felt normal. It was like I could be myself, without being ashamed or embarrassed. The Monster disappeared into darkness when he was around me.

My flip flops were covered in mud so I walked to the river and put my feet in the water to rinse them.

The water was calm and green, not muddy like the day I swam out to Slippery Rock. All was quiet except for the sounds of the river. The water was chattering, the birds chirping, and somewhere in the distance a frog croaked repeatedly.

I lifted my face to the sun and let the warmth soak through me. I closed my eyes, enjoying the moment. I smelled honey suckle and felt my mother brushing my hair.

It was quiet for a long time while I stood on the edge of the river. It seemed like the gang was giving me my space, like you do with an injured animal. You want to help it out, but you don't know if the animal is dangerous or not, so you wait and see before you help it.

"Ready?" Julie asked after a few minutes into my foot bath, breaking my meditative state.

"Yeah." I turned from the water and walked back to the gang.

We followed Julie to her house without talking. We entered, and her mother was in the same chair as last time. The TV was on and her back was to us.

"Mom, I'm home with some friends," Julie said. We were all standing at the entrance to the living room, waiting.

"Hi, Mrs. Thompson," I said. I even waved like a fool, knowing she wasn't going to turn around to greet us.

We went down the hallway and into Julie's bedroom. Wendy flopped down on the edge of Julie's bed. I sat in the makeup chair in front of the mirror.

Julie walked over to me and spun me around to face her. "Let's do your makeup."

I never knew anyone who loved doing makeup so much. I shrugged and said okay. Besides, I didn't have anything else to do.

Julie picked up the biggest brush from her tray and dabbed it into the powder. Then she put it to her lips and blew. Tiny speckles of the powder danced in the sun before floating to the ground. I loved the way the soft bristles felt like fingers caressing my face. I closed my eyes and imagined my mother. Felt her brush my hair that day in the front yard of our house.

"Keep your eyes closed."

Okay, Mom. Don't stop.

I felt a little pressure on my right eyelid as the tiny brush swept across it. Again and again. Then I felt the same thing on my left eyelid.

"I'm breaking up with Tommy," Julie said.

My eyes flew open. "What?" I asked. I was confused as to whether I heard her right.

"I'm breaking up with Tommy," Julie repeated. "As soon as the summer is over."

"Why wait until the end of summer?" Wendy asked. She was bouncing on the edge of the bed and seemed as confused as I was.

"Because." Julie said this as if we should already know why.

We sat there staring at her.

She realized we wanted an explanation, and put down the makeup and impatiently brushed back her hair with her hands. "Because, I can't go the rest of the summer *without* a boyfriend."

"But you and Tommy make a great couple," I said. I regretted it as soon as I said it. There were a lot of things I wanted to say but that was the stupid thing that came out of my mouth first. I realized she was conceited, but this was too much. I couldn't believe I tried to impress her by risking my life and swimming out to Slippery Rock and back.

Poor Tommy. He had no idea what was coming and I felt sorry for him. I also didn't want to be part of her dirty little secret.

Julie grabbed a tube of pink lip gloss and opened it. She put the tube down and held the applicator in front of my face.

She put her finger under my chin and lifted gently. "Be still." She swiped the spongy end of the applicator across my lips. They felt wet.

"And you two have been a couple ever since I can remember," Wendy said.

"Well, that's just it. I'm getting tired of Tommy. We *have* been together a long time . . . and now he's getting too possessive. I can't go anywhere without him asking me where I'm going. And he practically stares at any other boy who looks at me. The other day when I was life-guarding, he almost got into a fight with a guy that was just talking to me. And," Julie lowered her voice, "ever since I let him feel me up he wants to do it all the time."

I didn't know anything about her private life and her confession embarrassed me a little.

"I don't want him to get the wrong idea. He thinks I'm easy, and I'm not . . . Besides, my friend Anna said that her friend Trish told her that Joey Garcia likes me, and he was going to ask me to be his girlfriend when school started. He's so cute and he's on the track team, too. I'm so excited."

I saw Julie for the first time that day in her bedroom. Sure, she liked the attention of guys, but I really couldn't blame her about wanting to break up with Tommy now that I knew the real reason. Ever since I met Julie, I wanted to be like her, but now everything was different. And if I really thought about it, the times I was acting like Julie were the times that got me into the most trouble, were the times I got unwanted attention from Uncle Butch. I couldn't wait to be popular, but now, with everything that had happened over the summer, I just wanted to be a kid back in Virginia again. I wished I had never come here.

"Ta-da," Julie said. She turned me around to face the mirror.

When I saw my face and when I saw how grown up I looked, I gasped. Blue archways swooped across my eyelids and my lips were pink and heart shaped. I looked different, but not just different. I looked like an adult. I remembered what Julie said after the first time she put makeup on me. "You get noticed." Suddenly I realized what she meant. I saw what Uncle Butch saw in me. I wanted to die. I could never let him see me like this.

I jumped up from the chair and ran to the bathroom and closed the door. I turned on the cold water and lowered my face down near the faucet. I cupped my hands under the running water to catch it and then I splashed it on my face. Over and over. I looked up into the mirror, water dripping everywhere. My lip gloss was smeared onto the sides of my cheeks creating a clown's mouth. Blue eye shadow crept out of the corners of my eyes.

"Ugh!" I grabbed the bar of soap and put it under the water. I rubbed it between my hands generating enough suds to completely cover my face. I scrubbed until my eyes burned from the soap and then I splashed handfuls of water over my face until there wasn't any signs of make-up. Only then did I open the door.

Julie and Wendy were standing there, waiting.

"Why did you take the makeup off?" Julie asked with her "notice me" makeup on. She looked like her feelings were hurt.

"Uh . . ."

"Are you okay?" Wendy asked. She had blue eye lids, pink cheeks, and pink lips.

"I've got to get out of here!" I said as I pushed past them and left.

"You need to spend more time with your daughter!" I yelled at Julie's mother as I ran past her. Then I left as fast as I could.

Wendy ran after me. "Where are you going? Wait up." She trailed behind me.

As soon as we got back to the cottage, I pulled her by her arm to the kitchen sink. Luckily no one was around. "Wash it off."

"Why? What's gotten into you?"

"Just wash it off. It doesn't look good."

"What's wrong with you? You're acting like a crazy person. It's just makeup for Pete's sake."

"It's not just makeup. I want you to wash it off. It's like Julie said. You get noticed when you wear makeup, but you don't want Owl to get the wrong idea. Like Tommy did after feeling Julie up." I put the bar of soap in her hand and stood there until every last bit of the makeup was off her face and she was just my sweet innocent cousin again.

CHAPTER EIGHTEEN
SWEET REVENGE

BY FIVE O'CLOCK Thursday evening, everyone was at the back door of our cottage waiting for my command. Except for Paige, who was at Cody and Callie's cottage. I watched from the back door window and finally saw Uncle Butch disappear behind the shower curtain. I tapped Reds' shoulder excitedly. "Okay, he's in the shower. Let the snake out."

I opened the back door and moved the curtains from the window panel so we could see in. Then I closed the bathroom door so the snake wouldn't go in there. Straight ahead was the shower and behind the curtain was my uncle. Naked. Vulnerable.

I moved back so Reds could release our planned hell, and we watched as the snake poked its head out of the burlap bag. After a minute, it stopped moving, but I saw its forked tongue spit out, so I knew it was alive.

"Why isn't it moving?" I asked nervously. Tommy and Julie were standing off to the side holding hands. Little did he know that his time with Julie was limited. I felt sorry for him and his stupid grin. He looked so happy. How could Julie be so mean? But in my heart I knew now that meanness came from somewhere bone deep in a person.

Reds pushed at the burlap bag to coax the snake out further.

The shower curtain moved, and Reds jerked the burlap bag releasing the snake fully. I tugged on Reds' shirt for him to move away from the door. "Don't let my uncle see you."

Reds moved and I pulled the door closed.

Wendy and Owl went to the side of the house where the kitchen window was. They were on their tip toes looking in.

"Do you see anything?" I whispered.

"Mom's in the kitchen," Wendy said.

I looked back in toward the shower. "It's moving," I whispered. The plan was in motion, and there was no turning back.

Finally, the snake slithered toward the shower. It was slow at first and I waited while holding my breath. "Go into the shower," I said, almost willing it to move.

"You can't control a snake, Chris. Don't panic," Reds said.

"Finally! It's going toward the shower." I got goose bumps. The plan was working.

But it turned toward the kitchen instead of going into the shower.

Wendy gasped. "It's in the kitchen where my mom is." We all moved to the kitchen window to watch, barely seeing above the windowsill.

"Don't worry," Reds said mostly to calm down Wendy. "It's not poisonous. It's okay."

We heard Aunt Lori through the screen. Since it was summer, and very few people had air conditioning, most of the windows stayed open to let the breeze in. When there was a breeze.

"Quit it, Oreo. That tickles."

She swiped her kitchen towel at her feet as the snake slithered by her. "Oreo, leave me alone." The snake continued to pass by her ankles, and she finally looked down.

The snake lifted its head and stuck out its forked tongue. One hiss and Aunt Lori started screaming, "Butch, come here quick. There's a snake in the kitchen!" Careful to avoid the snake, she crept toward the shower, pulled open the curtain, and screamed, "Snake!"

We watched from the window, all struggling to see.

Uncle Butch appeared in the kitchen with a towel wrapped around his waist, dripping. He saw the snake and laughed. "Lori, it's just a harmless little snake. Nothing to be afraid of."

"Get it out of here; I *am* afraid." She climbed onto a chair, watching from a safer distance.

"Okay, take it easy." Uncle Butch disappeared. He reappeared with a broom in his hand. As soon as he hit the puddle on the kitchen floor, he slipped and fell, twisting his leg underneath him.

Wendy and Owl scattered, but I stayed by the kitchen window to see what was happening. Julie and Tommy walked off holding hands.

"Butch! Are you all right?" Aunt Lori leaned over him.

"Son of a bitch. My leg!" Uncle Butch said.

"Are you okay?"

"No! My leg," Uncle Butch yelled.

"What do you want me to do?" She sounded panicked.

"I need help getting up." He reached up with his hand and she tried to pull him up but it didn't work. He was just too heavy for her.

"Help, somebody!" She looked around and we all ducked.

"Lori, help me get some clothes on first," Uncle Butch said.

She disappeared into the master bedroom and returned with a pair of shorts and a T-shirt.

He took the shirt and pulled it over his head, but he couldn't get the shorts on past his ankles. "It's my knee. It hurts.

"Can you lift your legs up so I can pull them up?"

He lifted his legs in the air like a dead bug.

She inched them up to his hips. "Can you lift your butt so I can get them on?"

"I'm trying!"

She finally got the shorts on him and disappeared again.

I heard a knock and we walked to the front of the cottage. Aunt Lori was at the neighbor's door.

Within seconds, Bob came out of his cottage.

"Bob, I need your help."

"Lori? What is it?"

"A snake got into the cottage and Butch fell. He twisted his leg pretty good. I think he hurt his knee."

"Well, I guess we better get him to the hospital."

We followed Aunt Lori and Bob into the cottage. I watched from the porch.

Bob lifted Uncle Butch up by his shoulder and helped him to his feet. Aunt Lori supported his other shoulder. The three of them walked together onto the porch like a choreographed dance routine.

"Do you need help?" I asked as they passed by me. I had to force myself from smiling. This was actually way better than I had planned.

"No." Bob struggled to get Uncle Butch into the station wagon. With Reds' help, he finally got Uncle Butch into the back seat and then got in on the driver's side. Aunt Lori got in on the passenger's side and rolled the window down.

I watched from the porch. Wendy and Owl were standing by the car.

"Wendy, I have to take your dad to the hospital. Watch your sister until I get back." Bob didn't wait for an answer before he drove away in a cloud of dust.

I thought about the snake loose in the cottage and cringed. I hadn't really thought the whole thing through. "Reds?"

"Yeah?"

"We need to get the snake out of the cottage before it hurts someone else. It could even hurt Oreo," I said.

"Don't worry, it's not poisonous."

"Yeah, but we need to get it out of there." My fear was rising.

"Okay, okay. I'll go get it out right now," Reds said.

I smiled at him. "Thanks." I watched as he disappeared into the cottage on the hunt for the culprit.

Paige came out of Bob's cottage with Cody and Callie and came over to us. "What's going on?"

"A snake got in the house, and then Dad was trying to trap it, and well, it's a long story, but he twisted his leg," Wendy said.

"What if he broke it?" Paige asked.

"He didn't break it, just twisted it," I said.

I acted like I cared, but something had changed inside of me. I hoped he was as broken as I felt. I was Raggedy Ann, empty as my childhood doll, limp and sapped of life.

Wendy locked eyes with me and gave me one of those I-won't-tell-if-you-won't-tell looks and then I gave her an I'll-never-tell look. I was getting good at keeping secrets.

BY EIGHT O'CLOCK, they were back from the hospital. Uncle Butch had a bandage wrapped around his right knee and he was struggling with his crutches. He was lousy and clumsy with them, and as soon as he got inside the porch, he flopped into his chair, his crutches spilling off to the side.

"Well, that was an ordeal," Aunt Lori said, blowing her hair off her face and worrying around him. "Can I get you anything, Butch?"

"I'm starving. Do we have anything to eat?"

With that, Aunt Lori kissed his forehead, and went into the kitchen. "I'll whip you up something real nice."

Paige stood beside her dad, looking at the bandage. "Did it hurt?"

"Yeah," he said.

"I'm sorry you broke your leg, Daddy," Paige said, patting the top of his hand.

"I just twisted it, sweetheart, and I'll be okay," he said. "I hurt my knee a little, that's all."

Too bad for him. I shied away and sat at the kitchen table where I could see everyone and started playing Solitaire. Aunt Lori stirred a pot of macaroni and cheese while boiling hotdogs.

"Did you girls get anything to eat tonight?" she asked.

Wendy shouted, "No," from the porch, and I shook my head when Aunt Lori looked at me.

Paige walked into the kitchen. "How's Daddy going to walk with a hurt knee?"

"Oh, honey, don't worry about Daddy. It's just a little swollen and he can walk just fine. He has to get used to those crutches, though."

Wendy joined us in the kitchen. She leaned toward her mother, taking her into confidence. "What about the Fourth of July dance Friday night? Are we still going to be able to go?" She kept her voice low, but I could hear it from where I sat.

"Well, of course we'll go to the dance," she said to us, then raised her voice so Uncle Butch could hear. "Honey, don't you think you can at least go to the dance this Friday to watch?"

"Oh-my-God. The dance! How am I going to win the dance contest?" This seemed to be the first time he thought about it. I laughed inside and smiled my shit-eating grin.

Aunt Lori went to the porch and set the table. "Well, maybe it's time we let someone else win for a change." Her voice was sweet and understanding. "Honey, everyone here knows you're the best dancer. Alice and Bob are good at the jitterbug. They might even stand a chance if we're not entered."

"Alice and Bob? They prance around the dance floor like ducks flapping their wings."

"I'm just saying. I'm tired of entering the dance every year because we always win. Let someone else win."

"I don't want to let someone else win! It's the only thing I look forward to all summer."

"Keep your voice down."

When dinner was ready, he hopped over to the table, ignoring his crutches. For such a great dancer, Uncle Butch wasn't very coordinated without his dancing shoes. I smiled, happy in the knowledge that I put him out of commission, not only from hurting me again, but from dancing in the contest. The only thing I think he really loved. And I took it away.

CHAPTER NINETEEN
DANCE COMPETITION

IT WAS FRIDAY morning and we were on the porch enjoying the fresh air and sunshine. Uncle Butch couldn't drive so he gave his work number to Bob and told him to call and tell his work that he was sick.

He was sick all right, but his swollen knee didn't make it so.

"Tonight's a big night," Wendy said excitedly. "It's the bicentennial dance contest."

"Keep it down." Uncle Butch's voice was gruff.

She lowered her voice to a whisper. "I can't wait. I'm going to wear my blue shorts and my red-and-white striped shirt. I want to get into the spirit. What are you going to wear, Chris?"

"I guess I'll wear my blue shorts too. I have a white shirt, but I don't have any red. I don't know, I haven't thought that far ahead," I said.

"Don't worry, I'll find something red for you to wear. Besides, we have to look good for our dates," Wendy said.

"Dates? I told you not to hang out with those boys anymore!" Uncle Butch said. "Besides, aren't you girls a little young to be dating?"

Yeah, I was a little young for a lot of things, but that hadn't stopped him.

"Get with the program, Dad. All the girls have dates for the dance tonight. It's a dance contest and you have to have a partner to enter."

"Really? Well then, Wendy, who is your date?"

"Owl," Wendy said.

"Owl? That's a funny name," Uncle Butch said.

"I mean Max. Owl is his nickname," Wendy said.

"Chris, who is your date?" Uncle Butch asked. I felt his eyes on me, making me feel dirty.

"Wendy calls it a date. It's not." I didn't want to engage in this conversation with him.

"Well, then, who is your dance partner?"

"Dave," I said, using Reds' real name.

"The Johnson boy?"

I finally looked up and cut him a hard look. "Yeah, the Johnson boy. You know him, remember?" I asked with sarcasm.

I remembered. I remembered how he blew his hot breath into my ear. "I saw you dancing with that Johnson boy."

"Yeah, I remember him."

You're damn right you do! I got up from the couch and Wendy and Uncle Butch blurred red and yellow under the morning sun as I left the room.

"Chris, where are you going?" Wendy asked.

"Bathroom," I said over my shoulder.

I went into the little room with the stinking toilet, preferring to be in there than around him. I jammed both hands over my ears, drowning out any sound.

I finally re-emerged and heard the neighbor woman. "How you doing, Butch?" She was standing outside the porch.

"Hi, Alice. Doing okay," Uncle Butch said.

"I heard you got water on the knee."

"Yeah." He held up his crutches. "I've got to use these to get around." His voice had an edge.

"Well, we both hope you get better real soon. Maybe we'll see you at the dance later?"

"I don't know." His voice was harsh. Angry.

I smiled at Uncle Butch's suffering.

The teapot whistled. I heard the crutches tangle and the wood knock together as he tried to get up.

"Come on, Wendy," I whispered. "Let's get out of here. I need to thank Mrs. Weaver for Oreo." Paige was still sitting at the table. I mouthed to her so Uncle Butch wouldn't hear me. "Want to come?"

She nodded and we skedaddled out of there as fast as we could.

Cody and Callie were in front of their cottage. "Hey, Paige, are you going to decorate your bike for the parade tomorrow?" Their bikes were draped in red, white, and blue crepe paper. Cody was weaving the red roll in and out of the spokes of his bike's tire.

Callie threw her blue roll down into the basket on the front of her bike. "I can't do it."

Paige stepped closer. "Want me to help?"

"Sure," Callie said. Cody smiled big when Paige brushed by him to get to Callie's bike.

We left Paige with the twins and headed over to Crazy Mary's.

As soon as I saw the sun-washed cottage, I quickened my steps, eager to feed the cats. I looked under the sagging porch. A group of cats were huddled together in the shadow where the earth was still damp. Midnight's eyes glowed back at me like two little flashlights in the dark. Then we walked up the steps, sat down, and fed the other cats. Those that were brave enough to come up to us, that is.

Wendy talked about the dance. She could hardly contain her excitement. "I can't wait."

I was excited too. Not like her though. Her life hadn't been altered. Her monsters were still imaginary and lived under the bed. No. My excitement was about stopping A Monster. Taking something away from him like he did to me. I couldn't have planned a better prank. A better outcome.

I got lost in our conversation and was startled when the front door swooshed open.

"I thought I heard you girls out here." She had the sweetest voice.

"Hi." I stood up and brushed the back of my shorts off.

Wendy followed my lead and stood up too.

"I wanted to say thank you. You know, for Oreo."

She smiled and nodded. "Haven't seen you around in a while."

"We got into some trouble and were put on restriction."

"Everything okay now?"

"Yes."

"You take care of yourself and that little kitty. Cats can be a great comfort. And if you take care of them, they will take care of you."

I thought about cuddling with Oreo. About crying into his fur at night when everyone else was asleep. How he purred when I rubbed his head. That was my favorite sound in the world. It helped me push the demons out of my head so I could fall asleep. "I promise to take good care of him."

"Good. I knew you would. That's why I picked you to be his mama."

Mrs. Weaver's sweet voice telling me that she *chose* me made me want to cry. Then the thought of my own mother came rushing into my head. "I'll be a good mama."

She nodded.

"Come on. Let's go get ready for the dance." Wendy tugged my sleeve.

A FEW HOURS later we headed to the pavilion to meet up with our friends. Uncle Butch was still mad that he couldn't enter the dance contest and said he wasn't going. Aunt Lori knew we had plans so she told us to go ahead and they would meet us later. We left as fast as we could before she could change her mind.

It was the most beautiful place I had ever seen. Red, white, and blue bunting draped the entire structure of the porch on the outside. Replica lanterns from 1776 were hanging in a line around the pavilion and it was truly aglow. Red roses bloomed brightly around the perimeter and the contrast with the green grass was breathtaking. A banner hung over the entrance to the pavilion that read, "1776 to 1976, 200 years of Independence." Funny, it seemed like two hundred years since my mother dropped me off.

It was the biggest weekend of the summer at Shady Grove. People had gathered on the lawn. The music started up and we all started moving inside like ants to cake.

"Look at the tables!" I said.

They were covered in stars-and-stripes tablecloths, but they were made to look old-fashioned and worn, like they had actually covered tables in the Revolutionary times.

The dance floor quickly got crowded as the DJ played. I recognized a few faces. There was Dr. Ferguson and his wife, Cody and Callie's babysitter, and the black-haired girl. More importantly, I didn't see Uncle Butch and I felt relieved.

Reds whispered in my ear in a way that made me relax. "Come on, dance with me."

"Okay." The pounding of the drums made my heart quicken. We weaved through the crowd to the center of the room and found a little opening between dancing couples. Reds smiled and moved his hips while holding my hands. I followed his lead and soon we were dancing together. The more we danced, the better we got. Soon Julie and Tommy were next to us showing off their superior dancing skills. Wendy and Owl joined in too.

A new song came on. The only words I could make out were "shake your booty."

I saw Aunt Lori and Uncle Butch sitting at one of the tables by the door. Uncle Butch was holding his bottle wrapped in a brown paper bag. He sipped directly from it and pointed it toward us. Next to them was Bob and Alice and everyone was smiling and talking, except Uncle Butch who was pouting and putting a large dent in his bottle of whiskey. We of course had no whiskey because Freckles was not here, and besides, we were being watched closely. Plus, I didn't want to get into any more trouble.

Later, the announcer blew into the microphone and the speakers crackled. "It's time for everyone who entered the

Swing Dance Contest to please come to the concession stand and get your numbers."

We cleared the center of the dance floor and couples picked out prime real estate in front of the judges. The women pinned the numbers on the backs of the men's shirts and waited patiently. The music began and the contestants sprang to life. They danced full steam ahead, and it was glorious.

Alice and Bob shocked the crowd with an over-the-shoulder-and-through-the-legs move. Everyone clapped, including me. Other women let their skirts fly too, but not as impressively as Alice and Bob. Dr. Ferguson and his wife were showing off their fancy footwork and underarm turns too, but his weight slowed him down and he tired easily. I was increasingly impressed as the competition got fierce on the dance floor.

One judge walked around the dancers, watching. When he tapped the man's back, the couple had to leave the dance floor. Dancing couples dwindled until there were only two left, including Alice and Bob. I didn't know the other, but I'd seen them at the dances before.

After a few more dances, the music stopped. The announcer blew into the microphone. "Okay, folks. Let's give our contestants a round of applause. They did a great job." Everyone clapped, except Uncle Butch. "We will have a short break while the judges decide the winner from our two finalists." He pointed to the last two couples on the dance floor. Everyone clapped again.

Uncle Butch hobbled on one crutch out the door before they announced the winners. He was drunk and being a poor sport. Aunt Lori followed behind him, trying to help, but he just shooed her away. She motioned for us to come over to her, so we quickly said goodbye to everyone and left before we could find out who won.

IT WAS SATURDAY, and I was excited not for the festivities, but mostly because I knew that since Uncle Butch couldn't drive, Aunt Lori would have to take me to Mount Adams to call my mom. I felt free. It was my chance to escape. I jumped out of bed and ran straight for the kitchen where I found Aunt Lori starting breakfast.

"Good morning, sweetie. Your uncle is still asleep, so keep it down for a bit."

"Need any help?" I asked.

"No, honey, have a seat and drink some orange juice." I poured a glass from the pitcher on the table. "I thought we would take it slow this morning. Your uncle is not feeling very well. We'll go to the parade after lunch."

"When can you drive me to the house so I can call my mom?" I asked with anticipation.

"Oh, honey. I'm sorry. I don't drive."

Thunder struck my ears. I didn't think I heard her right. "What?"

"I don't drive."

How could I have not known? I thought about it. The trips to their house in Mount Adams to get clean clothes and fresh supplies, and the trips to the grocery store—it was always Uncle Butch who drove. And then there was the trip to the emergency room. It was Bob who drove. My mom drove everywhere and I couldn't imagine an adult who couldn't drive. I thought that Aunt Lori was just being a good wife by letting Uncle Butch drive everywhere. After all, she was that kind of woman.

"How am I going to call my mom?" I asked.

"I don't know, sweetie." She looked at me apologetically. "When your uncle gets up, we'll talk about it then, promise."

"She'll freak out if I don't call today," I said, my voice rising.

"I know. We'll figure something out. Maybe your uncle can drive you if his knee is not too swollen."

I said nothing. There was a fire burning in my stomach.

"I'll get the rest of the lazy bunch up," Aunt Lori said. She left and the smell of flowers drifted behind her. She went into the bedroom where Uncle Butch was still sleeping.

It was fifteen minutes before everyone was up and at the table. Uncle Butch stumbled in on his crutches, asking for aspirin. He sat down at the breakfast table across from me.

"Honey, do you think you can drive Chris to the house to call her mother?"

"I don't think so. But I'll take her as soon as I can drive again. Probably in a few days."

Not alone. That would never happen. I would rather hug a porcupine before going to the house alone with him. Or anywhere alone with him, for that matter.

"She'll be so worried if I don't call today."

Aunt Lori walked over to me and put her hand on my shoulder. "She'll understand. Promise." She should stop making promises she couldn't keep.

Uncle Butch stuffed aspirin into his mouth and grumbled. "I don't think I'll be going to the parade or the fireworks today. I feel more dead than alive."

"Aw, Dad," Paige whined. "You're not going to watch me in the parade?"

"Don't worry. I'll take you girls," Aunt Lori said. "I had a feeling your daddy wouldn't be feeling very good today. There's no reason you girls should miss the bicentennial events though. Two hundred years in the making. It's going to be fun, you'll see."

"Yay," Paige said.

Around one o'clock, we all left for the parade, except Uncle Butch. We dropped Paige and her decorated bike off at the staging area for the parade. We went to the viewing area where we found a place to stand next to Bob and Alice.

A few seconds later, Aunt Lori was getting the scoop about the dance contest. It was obvious that they had won by the way Alice was moving around. She was sort of bouncing up and down with her hands clasped together as if in prayer in front of her.

I saw the gang down the way and waved. Wendy waved too.

"Mom, can we go watch the parade with our friends?" Wendy asked.

"Okay, but don't go too far."

"Come on," Wendy said.

"Hey," Reds said and put his hand around my waist. Everyone else greeted us too, but my main concern was Reds.

We talked for a few minutes, but when we heard music, we turned to watch the parade. A band in red uniforms marched by. My favorite thing about a band were the drums, especially the big round ones that made such a loud boom it echoed in your heart.

The band was followed by straggling lines of kids riding their bikes, decorated in red, white, and blue. I saw Paige and the twins near the front. Paige waved and her handle bars swerved hard, almost knocking her off the bike. We waved back. The excitement was gaining momentum.

Next was a platform being pulled by a large truck that was full of Veterans dressed in military uniforms from all different wars. One man was in a wheelchair, smiling and waving at the crowd that had formed along the front of the pavilion's lawn. I almost cried when I noticed how proud they looked.

After the platform of Veterans, there was a walking formation of Revolutionary British soldiers in red coats, funny hats, and black boots. They were carrying long skinny rifles, the tip tucked up by their shoulders. They were followed by women in long dresses, who looked very hot. Behind them were the American soldiers and women following behind a large American flag. Some had uniforms but most didn't.

And at the end of the parade, two cannons were being pulled by farm tractors. We all clapped as the last of the parade walked by us and then dispersed onto the lawn.

After a few minutes I heard a loud whistle moan. "What was that?"

"It's the steamboat," Wendy said.

Everyone gathered behind the pavilion, where it overlooked the river from the hill and we all waited for the steamboat to get closer.

I caught sight of it, barely visible from around the bend. It got closer, and I saw the smokestack billow a dragon's breath that brought the boat to life. I had never before seen the beauty of a real paddleboat, and I knew I would always remember it. I could hear the roar of water churning as a great wheel on the back thrust the boat forward chopping the water into a furious froth.

I could make out the faces of some of the passengers who were smiling and waving at the gathering crowd behind the pavilion. I wondered where they came from or where they were going. I listened to the song of the travelling water and it lured me into a fantasy where I was one of the passengers, ready for a new adventure, one far away from here. I could smell the cherry tobacco of a man's pipe and could see the sparkle of a woman's diamond ring, or so I imagined.

After the steamboat paddled out of sight, we followed the crowd back out front onto the lawn. A huge barbecue grill was on the side of the pavilion with hotdogs scattered over it, and Cincinnati chili was next to it in a big pot. Two men were manning the grill and several women were around a table next to it, getting the condiments and buns ready. There was also a big bowl of baked beans and a large orange cooler full of lemonade.

About a hundred people were gathered at the pavilion already, mostly on the lawn where the food beckoned hungry bellies.

We stood in a short line for a chili dog and baked beans. Then we got our lemonade, which was too sweet, but we drank it anyway.

We wandered over to the edge of the pavilion where the pine trees were and found some privacy and some shade away from the growing crowd. We sat down in a circle, sitting crossed legged with our plates in our lap as we ate. Reds sat next to me.

"How do you like the Cincinnati chili, Chris?" Reds asked.

"It's really good," I said, wiping chili from my mouth with my napkin.

After we ate, Julie stood up and wiped the back of her shorts off. "Looks like the re-enactors are getting ready to put on their show. Let's go over and see what's happening."

The re-enactors were forming on the front lawn. The British soldiers were on the left and the American soldiers were on the right. Each group had a cannon facing its enemy. Their rifles were straight up and down against their shoulders as in waiting. All was quiet in anticipation. Then the command was given by Colonel Saunders.

"Fire!"

In a flash, the soldiers were storming one another, their rifles pointed at the hearts of their enemies. Men from both sides were in hand to hand combat for about fifteen minutes.

Next, a cannon went off, and smoke covered the right half of the battlefield. Another bang, and more smoke followed. It looked as real as if it had been 1776 and we were standing right in the middle of the action, fighting for our freedom. Soldiers fell to their re-enacted deaths one by one until a small band of American soldiers declared victory over the British. Everyone clapped and cheered until all of the *dead* soldiers were up and walking off the battlefield.

The smoke cleared, and I saw an elderly woman standing beside a man in a wheelchair. The man had on a dark green uniform with a matching tie. He was missing both legs from the knee down. Across his chest were two lines of medals, but the one I noticed most was the purple one hanging from a ribbon and the medal was heart shaped. I guess purple didn't make everything seem more exciting, didn't always mean that your life might someday become a Broadway musical.

I felt bad for the man in the wheelchair. I still had my legs, yet I felt like I couldn't move. Couldn't escape.

The man saluted the flag with bravery only a soldier could do. His eyes were sad and watery. I thought about what horrors he must had to face in the war, and yet he still saluted the flag. Then it hit me. Freedom had been declared and it took a whole country to fight for it. We were celebrating two hundred years of it. Like everyone who fought for their freedom before me, I would join them.

"Reds?"

He turned to me. "Yeah?"

"Do you know why I wanted to pull that prank on my uncle?"

"It's because he put you on restriction, right?"

I had to navigate cautiously. "Yeah, that's some of it, but there's more to it than that."

"What?"

I paused, trying to gather my bravery.

He nudged me. "You can tell me. I'll protect you."

I thought of the fight at the beginning of summer and how he tried to break it up. I believed him. "Well, it's because he's mean too. Especially when he's drinking. Which is every night."

"Freckles' Dad is an alcoholic, and he's pretty mean too."

He was getting off the subject. I tried again.

"Yeah, well, he's not just mean. He's a bad man."

"What do you mean? Has he hit you?"

Just then, the elderly gentleman in the white suit took the microphone and blew into it, making a loud hiss.

Reds looked over at the man, then back at me, waiting for an answer. But I couldn't talk over the microphone.

"Next, we will have the three-legged race. Everyone interested needs to come to the steps of the pavilion to get your leg ties. You will then stand at the starting line over there and tie your legs together." He pointed to the side of the pavilion where there were a couple of women waving.

Reds tucked his hand into mine. It was warm and gentle. "Okay. Now. You were saying he hit you? I swear I'll hurt him if he's touched you."

This is not what I wanted to happen. I didn't want Reds to go off starting a fight with my uncle. Violence wasn't the answer. Getting home safe was the answer.

"No, wait. I didn't say he hit me. He's just mean is all. Just forget about it." I wanted to drop it, so I thought of a quick exit strategy. "Do you want to be partners in the three-legged race?"

"Yeah, sure."

We went to the front of the pavilion where the crowd was gathering. He was still holding my hand and I knew he was still thinking about what I had just told him. I squeezed his hand to reassure him that I was okay.

After we got our leg ties, we walked over to the starting line and met up with Paige, who was tying her right leg to Callie's left leg. She giggled when she saw us. Reds tied his leg to mine and we stood next to Julie and Tommy. Owl and Wendy were next to them and we all struggled to stay upright with our arms around each other. There were sixteen couples, both young and old. Aunt Lori and Alice were on the sidelines cheering us on. A man at the beginning of the line held up a starter gun.

Reds and I leaned forward, waiting. A second later the gun went off. We hobbled down the grassy lane, trying not to fall into one another, walking as fast as we could for the finish line. We had our arms around each other's waist, walking first with our free leg, then moving as one unit with the legs that were tied together. We developed a kind of hop and a skip but we finally found our rhythm. We were tied for first place with Julie and Tommy.

I ran faster, taking Reds with me. Just as we were about to cross the finish line, Julie bumped into my shoulder. She was pushing me, trying to knock me off balance. I pushed back but it wasn't enough to get her away from me. We were tied with just a few more hops before we finished. Julie's foot jutted out in front of me, causing me to lose my balance. We stumbled and by the time we found our rhythm again, Julie and Tommy crossed the finish line before us.

Reds and I came in right behind the black-haired girl and her partner, and we fell in the grass, legs still tied together, laughing. We were sweating on each other and I was acutely aware of his leg against mine.

"We won," Julie said with her hands up in the air. She chose a stuffed bear as her prize and she walked around with that thing like she was a queen.

I looked at her with a sideways glance. "Cheater," I said, but no one heard me but Reds, who gave me a knowing smile.

"We'll get them next time," Reds said. "And we won't have to cheat to win."

Wendy walked up to us. "Let's go back to the cottage before the fireworks. I have to use the bathroom."

Julie overheard and took over as usual. "Yeah, me too. Let's take a break and meet back here around seven to watch the fireworks." She looked around at everyone. "Sound good?"

As her loyal subjects, we all nodded silently.

Back at the cottage Uncle Butch was sulking in his chair. It was a little after four.

Paige was sitting on the couch, playing with Wendy's Barbie doll.

Aunt Lori came out to greet us. "Having fun, girls?"

"Having a great time," I said, sitting next to Paige, placing her between me and Uncle Butch. Wendy sat on the other side so that now I had them both as a buffer.

"You're missing everything, Daddy," Paige said.

Uncle Butch nodded at Paige, but he didn't smile. His eyes washed over me in a way that made me feel like I needed a shower. I was ashamed of myself when he looked at me, his eyes exploring every inch of my body. I had long given up wearing the dresses that Wendy had lent me in exchange for my own tomboy clothes, but that didn't matter to him.

He was quiet. Then, as if trying to figure something out, he asked, "How do you suppose a snake got into the cottage?" His tone was accusatory. He was staring at me, even though Wendy and Paige were sitting right next to me.

His face seemed to be caving in on itself, like a pug dog. He paused after every few words. His question sounded like: "How . . . do you suppose . . . a snake . . . got into the cottage?"

I guess he had all afternoon alone to think about it. He was a regular mathematician, putting two and two together like that. Or as Lisa would say, a "math-magician." Yeah, he was a regular Sherlock Holmes. I knew I would pay if he ever found out I was the master mind behind the snake prank. And I didn't want to know what he'd do if he found out.

Wendy gave me a worried look. I thought about it for a minute. How were we going to get out of this one? But my anger matched his.

"I don't know . . . Uncle Butch. Maybe the way all snakes get anywhere. It crawled in."

"You better watch yourself, young lady."

"Yeah, that's what I'm trying to do." I walked into the kitchen, feeling victorious and scared at the same time. I knew I had just poked the bear.

CHAPTER TWENTY ONE
FIREWORKS

I WAS ANXIOUS THE rest of the afternoon, waiting for it to get late enough to go to the fireworks. To put some distance between me and The Monster.

Finally, the time arrived and at seven, Wendy and I left the cottage to meet up with the gang. Everyone was there except Julie, but I didn't care. I felt anxious when she was around. We all jockeyed for the best position on the grass in front of the pavilion. Tommy saved a seat next to him for Julie and I felt sorry for him again. But maybe he shouldn't have felt Julie up and then pressured her to do more. I had the urge to tell Reds a couple of times but every time I started to tell him, I got interrupted.

Over a hundred people scattered across the lawn waiting for the fireworks. I felt the excitement rise up inside me. I was fully aware that Reds' leg was touching mine as we sat crossed-legged beside each other. I didn't know whether to move my leg away from his or not. It was one of the few times I had seen him without his baseball cap and his loose curls outlined his face. I thought he looked cute.

He smiled and put his arm around my waist, but it wasn't enough for him. He leaned over and kissed me. I panicked. Would it ever be enough for him? What if he wanted what Uncle Butch wanted? More than just a kiss. Don't guys always want more? Like Tommy with Julie. I knew what the "more" was and I wanted no part of it.

But I liked Reds. And he was gentle. And I liked his kiss.

He reached for me, but not in the urgent way of Uncle Butch. He took my hand into his own, interlocking them like a puzzle piece. It was as if he was trying to put me back together again.

A few minutes later Julie showed up. "Hey you guys," she greeted everyone, then looked at Reds and me and smiled. "Don't you two look cute together." She plopped down next to Tommy, waiting for the night to turn dark.

After fifteen minutes as the sky darkened, Alice and Aunt Lori walked up to our circle with the kids in tow.

We stood up to greet them. Cody, Callie, and Paige were bathed in the light of their sparklers. I smelled the burning and heard the sizzle of the sparklers, and when they sparked out, Aunt Lori lit six more for them. They had one in each hand and were circling them around in front of them, lighting up our faces in the growing darkness. The fire was fascinating, a spectacular show, sparking and flaming in the darkness like an actress mesmerizing her audience.

Off in the distance, firecrackers exploded and it sounded like gunfire. Everywhere I looked, groups of people were waiting. Most of them had sparklers or firecrackers. In the darkness and surrounded by people, I felt a sense of peace, standing next to Reds. He leaned into me and squeezed my hand. In that moment, I saw my reflection in his eyes. I wasn't the girl I saw reflected in the darkness of Uncle Butch's eyes. He looked at me as if I had angel wings, like I was someone to be adored.

The fireworks started, and my sense of peace gave way to excitement. Dozens of sparkling circles appeared in many different colors, and a loud boom followed that echoed in my heart. The sky lit up with dozens of flowering dandelions. No sooner had they started to disappear, another batch of blooms shot up into the sky.

The fireworks were like a spectacular flashlight shining down on my heart. A memory rushed into my head. A memory I didn't want and couldn't shake. The fireworks looked just like the dandelion puffs I blew at my dad when

I was little. The thought of me never saying goodbye to him stung me. I tried to push the memory out of my mind but I couldn't. I'm too old to blow dandelion puffs now, but if I ever saw him again, I would tell him how much I loved that memory. How much I loved him. And even though I was still mad at him for leaving, he was a way better father than Wendy's. And if Wendy ever found out what her father did to me, we would both be fatherless. That made me sad. Made me worry that I was becoming like my mother.

"Look, Mom," Paige said, pointing up.

"Isn't it beautiful, honey?" Aunt Lori said.

After twenty minutes, explosions boomed one after the other as the whole sky lit up before us. I felt a quick thrill as the finale enveloped me, the booms bursting in my heart. The booms echoed in my chest so strong it felt like a revolution was forming inside of me. It was as if the noise bouncing around in my chest had restarted my heart, a charge coursing through my veins.

Red's face was glowing from the bright lights, and he never looked more beautiful. In that moment, I was just a girl with a crush on a boy. I thought of nothing else but him. Not the look on Uncle Butch's face when he was sweating above me. Not the sound of Aunt Lori singing her song of denial, nor the shadows that haunted my mother.

I wasn't going to let Uncle Butch define me anymore.

I was going to Be Brave and declare my independence.

TUESDAY ARRIVED, AND Uncle Butch's knee was better and he could drive to work again. He still limped around a little but he was walking on it all the same.

After work, Uncle Butch came into the porch. The first thing he said was, "I'm going to take Chris to the house so she can call her mother." It was like he had been thinking about this moment all day.

The bear wanted revenge.

"Only if Wendy comes with me," I said. There was an edge to my voice, which made Aunt Lori stop what she was doing.

Before Uncle Butch could object, Aunt Lori said, "That's a good idea. As a matter of fact, we'll all go and we can stop at White Castle for dinner."

"Yay!" Paige said. "I love White Castle."

"What? I don't think that's a good idea," Uncle Butch said, his smile gone.

"Yes, we're all going. I don't feel like cooking and I'm dying to get out of this cottage. There are a few things I need at the house too." She looked at Paige. "Get your shoes on, honey."

The three of us girls crowded into the back seat and Aunt Lori got in on the passenger side. It took longer than the usual fifteen minutes because of traffic and I was glad when we finally got to the house. I stretched my legs out a few seconds before going inside.

Aunt Lori and Uncle Butch were in the kitchen. I didn't see Wendy or Paige, but the TV was on. I picked up the phone and called my mom.

"Chris!" she exclaimed. "Why didn't you call me on Saturday? I've been so worried."

"Yeah, well, that makes two of us." I was getting a smart mouth and I wasn't the only one who noticed. Aunt Lori and Uncle Butch noticed too. They stopped what they were doing and looked at me. Especially Uncle Butch. I was glad he was noticing. I wanted to put a scare into him.

"Is everything all right?" Her words were hurried, her breaths were quick.

"Mom. Calm down. Everything is fine. I couldn't call on Saturday because Uncle Butch hurt his knee and couldn't drive me to the house."

"Is he okay?"

"Yeah, he's fine. But he couldn't drive until today." I paused. I knew they were listening but I just didn't care anymore. "Mom, I want to come home. I mean it. I'm not pussy-footing around anymore."

"Chris? This doesn't sound like you."

Aunt Lori busied herself by collecting food from the kitchen cabinets while Uncle Butch popped open a beer. He leaned against the kitchen counter, watching me with The Evil Eye. I know they were both still listening.

I needed to proceed with caution or else I would get the sausage finger across the neck too.

"Yeah, Mom. It does sound like me. I've been telling you all summer I want to come home, but you're not listening. You need to listen to me now. Got it?" I knew I sounded terse but I didn't know how else to get through to her.

"What has gotten in to you?"

I backed down a little. I still felt bad for her after all. "Nothing, Mom. I'm just really worried about you. And Dad."

"What makes you bring up your dad, sweetie? He'll be home soon."

God. I didn't know which was worse with their denial. My mom or my aunt.

"I know about the divorce, Mom. Uncle Butch told me."

Aunt Lori cut a look at Uncle Butch. He glared at me. I was what my mom called, "walking a thin line."

"He did, did he? Don't believe everything you hear. I'm still working on it."

Well, I hope she was working on getting rid of that secretary that he always seemed to be taking his business trips with. That would be a start. She also needed to work on finding him a new job that would keep him home more. Then she needed to work on not being so depressed all the time so he would want to stay home in the first place. But that would take miracles. I didn't see it happening.

"Okay. Just work on coming to get me, too. Okay?"

"Okay, honey. I will. I love you."

After I hung up the phone, Wendy yelled from the family room, "Chris, come here."

No way. I didn't want to feel the fabric of the couch as it scratched my bare skin and I didn't want to see that damned photograph that burned my eyes out.

"No, Wendy. It's time to go eat dinner," Aunt Lori said. Then she turned to me. "Sweetie, I didn't know you wanted to go home so badly. We'll have a talk soon, okay?"

I nodded and I knew it shook Uncle Butch to death when he heard it because it shook me too.

CHAPTER TWENTY THREE
THE RIVER RUNS RED

WE GOT BACK as the sun was setting. Aunt Lori didn't bring up The Talk, so we went to the game room to meet up with our friends like we did most nights.

We played pinball while the guys played pool. The radio was on, but I wasn't in the mood for music. It just seemed to break my heart now.

I had the right flipper and Wendy had the left as we tried to get that crazy silver ball back up to the top of the game to score more points. Lights were flashing and bells were ringing. I leaned into the game and moved my body in the direction I wanted that ball to go, but we still lost.

Julie was going to meet us after her job of life-guarding. She pushed through the screen door in a hurry. She was still in her red one piece bathing suit. "I guess you're not worried about your uncle," Julie said, panting.

"What do you mean? He's at the cottage," I said.

"Really? I just saw him walking toward the river. He had your kitten in his arms," she said.

"Wait . . . What?" I asked. It took me a second to process.

"He was carrying Oreo."

"But why was he going toward the river?" I asked. Oh God, he was going to get his revenge after all.

There was a short silence between us before reality hit me. I panicked. What if he was really going to drown Oreo? "I have to save him," I yelled.

I raced to the river without waiting to see if the others followed. I ran like my mother, I ran like I was running a marathon. I would never forgive myself if I let Uncle Butch drown Oreo—just as I knew I would never forgive him for stealing *home* from me.

By the time I reached the top of the path that led to the river, Uncle Butch was returning. I ran directly toward him. The brush closed in around us and we were barely visible from the cottages. The sky was blood-stained and his face was pinned to the fireball hanging above us.

I broke into a thousand pieces, each fragment screaming. *Okay, I say it. I give in. I say Uncle! Are you happy now?*

"What did you do with him?" I asked, pounding my fists on his chest.

"Aren't you a feisty one," Uncle Butch said, grabbing my hands. He forced my hands behind my back. His hands were like chains against my skin, pulling me down. Then he kissed me on the mouth. His lips were wet, and his teeth scraped against mine.

I struggled, trying to release myself from his grasp, but he overpowered me. I leaned away from him, trying to pull him off balance. When that didn't work, I was enraged. I squirmed and screamed, "No!"

He laughed at me, and I fought harder, but my strength was no match for his. I continued to squirm, determined not to let him have his way with me anymore. My anger was blinding me.

Suddenly, I fell back and my hands were free. Reds was standing behind Uncle Butch, holding a big tree limb. Evidently he had hit him with it.

I regained my balance and kicked Uncle Butch between his legs. "I'm going to tell everyone what you did to me!"

Then I saw it. The realization in Reds' eyes. It only took a second, but I knew he had figured it out. I could see all his emotions: the hurt, the fear, the pain. He looked at me, and I was no longer the angel he saw during the fireworks. I knew right then that I would never fit into his perfect penny world. I would always be the flattened penny that my mom gave me, something different than what I used to be.

Reds held the tree limb like he was ready to swing a baseball bat. His face was the color of ripe tomatoes and his knuckles were white from holding the branch so tight. He swung the branch at Uncle Butch and I heard a whack as part of it splintered off and flew past me, just missing my head. He didn't even notice the near collision because he was so focused on beating my uncle repeatedly across the back with the branch.

Every time Reds took a swing at him, Uncle Butch screamed, "No! Stop!"

The same words I had said to him.

A few minutes later, the rest of the gang appeared. Wendy saw me crying and her Dad bent over and beat up, I could tell her loyalties seemed divided.

Tommy took the branch away from Reds and pushed him back a little while the rest of the gang surrounded him, blocking him from Uncle Butch.

Oreo popped into my head. I ran as fast as I could toward the river, toward the horizon, leaving everyone behind in confusion.

I walked to the river's edge and searched for Oreo.

I yelled for all I was worth. "Oreo! Or-ree-oh!"

I followed the line of the bank in case he washed up. It was empty. The water tempted me. Muddy and maddening, it had its own way of speaking to me.

The water lapped at the edge of the shoreline, pulsing in and out as regular as a beating heart. The waning sun painted the sky red and bled into the water. I heard the crickets hum in the warm summer air. It was quickly turning dark. My anxiety got worse as I searched for my kitten. I wasn't a good mama any more.

I saw Oreo floating by, but as my vision became clearer, Oreo turned into a log. I was relieved, but still uncertain of his safety.

I walked to the river's edge where I stripped my shoes and socks off. I put my feet in the cold water and my feet disappeared into the muddy bottom.

Tears filled my eyes and dropped into the river. The water absorbed my fear and carried it away, and the recent events washed from my mind. I turned, travelling with the current, letting it take me as I searched for Oreo.

I swam further out, and I reached down with my foot to see if I could touch bottom. A shooting pain entered me and crawled up my leg, burning. I stepped on something. I couldn't get it out of my foot, whatever it was. I had to get to Slippery Rock if I was going to release it. I swam hard, fighting to get a grip on the moss-covered rock. Finally, I found a crevice to hold on to and I pulled myself out of the water.

I brought my foot up and pulled the thing from my heel. I had to pull hard because a shard of glass had lodged deep in my flesh. As I pulled it out, blood flowed from the cut and washed away in the current of the river. It felt good, this cut on my foot. I examined the glass, watching the dimming light reflect through it. If even a drop of his poisonous blood was inside of me, then I didn't want it.

Before I could stop myself, I took the jagged edge of glass and put it against my arm. I heard Uncle Butch's voice, "This never happened."

I pulled down quickly, creating a deep cut. I watched the blood swirl in the current and then disappear.

It would have been enough for this to end the pain, but I cut repeatedly. It finally felt good to release the pain that was locked up inside of me.

I let go of the rock and let the water take me on its serpentine journey.

I remembered the morning I was baptized. Christianity came from the water, cleansing my soul. Now, in the river, I finally felt cleansed again as I floated first face up, then the current rolled me over and buried my face in the water. I surrendered to the river.

Then everything went black. There was no standing ovation, no applause. Just the curtain closing, and the fading into darkness.

CHAPTER TWENTY FOUR
FREE AT LAST

I HEARD A tapping sound. It sounded like nails being hammered into my coffin.

"Come in," a woman's voice said.

"Doc, glad you're here."

"Okay, Mary. Let me have a look here." The doctor's voice was calm, deep. He lifted my leg to examine the cut on the heel of my foot. Next, he examined my arm, wiping away the blood with a wad of gauze. He put his glasses on and looked closer. "No way she got these from the river," he said in a low voice, but I could still hear. "Only some need sutures."

I felt the prick of the needle on the bottom of my foot, and then the liquid bubbled under my skin in a tight ball. When the numbness set in, I only felt a faint tingle as the thread was laced around the wound. I felt the same thing on my arm and I passed out again.

SLOWLY I WOKE to the smell of soap and lavender. I couldn't feel the rhythm of the river any more. Long fingers of light reached down and teased my eyelids until I could no longer keep them shut. A white bandage was wrapped around the cuts on my arm and on the bottom of my foot. The tightness felt good, like it would keep me from splitting into a thousand pieces. I scanned the room and didn't recognize anything, but I felt safe in its warmth. A blanket was tucked around me like a cocoon.

I entered the river a child ready to die, but was saved by the most unexpected angel.

Just as I thought about her, she entered the room with a serving tray full of food and hot tea. She sat the tray on the bedside table. I couldn't believe how hungry I was.

There was hot tomato soup made with milk, not water, and a grilled cheese sandwich made with thick deli bread and real cheddar cheese. There was a cupcake with chocolate icing. A tea bag was draped over the side of a mug decorated with butterflies.

Comprehension came in a rush. "Where's Oreo?"

"You needn't fuss about Oreo. He's a strong kitten. We found him washed up on the shore a few feet from you."

"He's alive?" I felt a rush of relief and guilt at the same time. Mrs. Weaver chose me to take care of him and I failed.

"Yes. He's with his mother, resting. There's nothing like a mother's love to make one strong again."

That was true and I felt horrible that I wasn't a good mama to Oreo.

She sat on the edge of the bed. "Eat some soup while I talk to you. It's been a good while since I've had company."

I spooned soup in my mouth like I had never tasted food before.

I had a chance to look at her real good for the first time. She marked time through her wrinkles, deep thoughtful wrinkles on her face. She wet her fingers to tame her long cotton candy hair that was pulled back into a bun. She patted my hand with hers, and it felt like a velvet glove. The hair on my arm rose joyously at her touch. "You are a survivor, something I know a little about myself." Before I could say anything, she put her finger to her lips. "Shhh, you rest. I'll talk." She seemed to be able to read my mind. "I know what everybody says about me. I know my nickname is Crazy Mary—"

"I'm sorry—"

"No, no need for apologies. I don't mind it so much. A person gets used to things in order to survive. For me, the name signifies all that I had to go through to get to this point in my life. Before my husband died, I was just Mary, wife, and friend. I prefer the nickname because in a sense, Mary died and Crazy Mary took her place.

"I saw you on my porch, curious and fluttering around this place like a butterfly. I knew they told you about me, the rumors I mean, but you didn't let that stop you. I saw you come every day with your cousins with food for the cats. I saw you clean the weeds out of my flowerpots and put flowers in them. I saw a spark in you.

"I feel . . ." I struggled to explain it. "I feel different." I rubbed the bandage on my arm.

"Don't worry, I don't judge, honey. We all have our scars to carry with us. Scars are a sign of bravery," she paused, "of survival."

"I don't know why . . . I mean, do you just ever feel like words aren't enough?"

She smiled and the sparkle in her eyes matched the stars I saw in the river the first day I saw it. "Yes."

"Does my cousin know I'm here?"

"Yes. She came by earlier to check on you. Said she told her parents you were okay."

"I don't want to ever go back to my uncle's place."

"I know. The doctor said you should remain here for a while, and I agree. I don't know how much of this you want to keep private or how much you want them to know. But know this. If you let them, secrets can break you into a thousand pieces. You're a strong girl and you will get through this. Understand?"

I nodded.

"Now, I guess you need to call your folks and let them know what's happening."

Oh God. Mom. How was I ever going to tell her what happened?

"I need to get to a phone. Not the one at my uncle's house either."

"Sure, honey. I have a phone downstairs in the kitchen."

"What?" I thought of all those times I had to fight the monster just to talk to my mother. My stomach emptied out through my feet. "You have a phone?" I started sobbing. I couldn't believe there was a phone so close. If I had known, I could have been saved. I could have called my mom and told her the truth. Told her to come get me without Uncle Butch listening in on my conversation and hovering over me and threatening me. I couldn't stop crying.

"What is it? Are you okay?"

"I'm okay," I said between sobs, trying to breathe. "I . . . didn't . . . know."

"It's okay. You call whenever you're ready."

"How am I going to tell my mom?"

"Set the truth free and you will be free too."

"But what if I had told . . . ?"

"Don't play that 'what if' game, it will drive you crazy. 'What if' I had been with my husband the day he died? 'What if' I had been there instead of him? Believe me, I spent years playing that game and I became the most miserable person you'd ever want to meet." She took my face in her hands and looked directly in my eyes. "You didn't do anything to cause this to happen to you." She said it so sincerely that I started to believe her.

I got out of bed and immediately a pain shot up from the cut on my foot. I lifted my heel and walk-limped to her and hugged her. I had on a long nightgown which I figured belonged to Mrs. Weaver. It was as delicate as her touch, flowery and lacy. So unlike me.

She hugged me back.

"Okay, I'm ready to call." I was broken and only my mother's love could put me back together.

I followed her downstairs and into the kitchen, taking in all the rooms we passed. It certainly wasn't a house of a crazy person and it didn't seem haunted at all. It was a house full of love and light.

There was a yellow phone hanging on the wall that matched the wallpaper. It reminded me of lemons. Of my mom. Fresh squeezed lemons plus sugar and water equaled my mother. She always told me that if life gave you lemons, make lemonade. It seems my dad leaving gave us both a lot of lemons. Between us, we would be making lemonade the rest of our lives.

"I'll leave you alone."

I dialed the numbers that would connect me to my mother with trembling fingers. I was nervous. I hoped I could unearth my mother from her darkness. Make her understand.

"Hello?"

"Hi, Mom."

"Chris? Why are you calling so late? Is everything all right?"

I filled my lungs with air to steady myself. Then I let out a deep breath. "No, Mom. Everything is not all right. I need you to come get me."

"Oh my God. What is it? Are you hurt?"

"No. Yes. But everything is okay now. You just have to come get me."

"Oh, honey. What is it?" She started crying.

"Mom, you're just going to have to trust me on this. I need to come home."

More crying. "Why? What is it?"

"I'll tell you everything when you get here."

She exhaled and sniffed. "Are you sure you're not hurt?"

"Well, I had to have a few stitches for some cuts, but I'm okay."

"Stitches?!"

"Yes, but please don't panic. I'm going to be fine."

"I'm so worried."

"Will you come and get me?" That was the question I wanted to ask her all summer.

I imagined her on the other end of the phone gathering her bravery. "Of course I will. You hold tight honey. I'll leave first thing in the morning."

"You have to pick me up at Mrs. Weaver's house. The big house on the edge of Shady Grove."

"Where?"

"Mary Weaver's house."

"Crazy Mary? The Cat Lady?"

I cringed. She was my savior and she certainly wasn't crazy. It was just a horrible nickname Uncle Butch gave her. "Yeah."

"Why are you there?"

I had to think fast. "It's where the doctor stitched me up. I have a cut on my foot and it's hard to walk." I paused, thinking about my family tree and all that was left of it. A stump. "We're going to be okay, Mom. We are family now, just the two of us. And we will survive." I didn't know who I was trying to convince more, me or her. But I held on to that belief.

"What do you mean? Where is your uncle?" There was a tremble in her voice.

"Everything's fine. You've got to be brave for me now. Can you do that?"

She exhaled as if she had taken all the air out of the room. "Yes."

I said goodbye and after I hung up the phone, I put my head against the wall to gather my strength. I couldn't wait to see my mother again, but it was going to be bitter sweet. A few minutes later I limped back upstairs.

Mrs. Weaver came to the door. "Everything okay?"

I nodded. I was too exhausted to speak.

She turned off the light and a wave of lavender brushed across me as she left. I knew I was safe in her house and I felt at peace for the first time in weeks. I drifted into sleep with thoughts of being home.

"CHRIS, WAKE UP." Wendy's voice drifted into my sleeping thoughts.

In my dream, she had on a captain's uniform and was steering the paddleboat, waving me on board.

"Chris, wake up." She put a squirming Oreo on my chest. The tickle of his whiskers against my face woke me instantly.

"Hey," I whispered.

"Heard you nearly drowned in the river, again. We were all so worried when you ran off like that."

"Wendy? What are you doing here?"

She handed me a sunflower. "I came to see you."

"I hope you're not mad at me," I said. I took the flower and put it on the bedside table.

She hugged me. "Don't you know that I look up to you? You're my best friend."

I felt my cuts burning. Throbbing. I sat up in bed and hugged her. "I'm sorry. I'm so sorry for everything." I should have said something more but couldn't. I felt guilty.

"Do they hurt?"

I repeated what she had told me about her scar. "It did at first but it doesn't anymore. It's just a reminder now." I smiled weakly.

"You did it to yourself, didn't you?" Wendy asked.

Her question surprised me. I couldn't talk for a minute. "How did you know?"

"Because I know why you did it."

I couldn't respond. I just sat there not knowing what to say. What exactly did she know?

"I can't believe he tried to drown Oreo."

Well, that explained it. I wanted to tell Wendy the truth. Tell her what really happened, but I didn't want to share that with her just yet. Maybe I would write it all down someday.

"I hate him. I get so mad, I can't even think. I just feel like I want to break something." She took a deep breath.

After she left, I crawled out of the cocoon of covers and got out of bed, careful not to put any weight on my heel. I spotted my clothes on the chair. They were washed and neatly folded.

I stood up on rubber band legs and walked over to the mirror. I looked at myself. I was ghost white. Shadows crept over my sunken eyes. There were ugly things reflecting back at me.

After I changed into my clothes, I heard voices downstairs.

I met Mrs. Weaver as she was coming up the steps. "What's going on?" I asked.

"The police are here, honey. But don't be afraid. The police officer is questioning witnesses and such about yesterday. He wants to talk to you."

I heard Reds. "I was running as fast as I could, but boy, can she run. I caught up to her at the path and when I saw the two of them together, I couldn't control myself. He was hurting her. He had her hands pinned behind her back. I ran straight for him and started punching. I couldn't stop. When that didn't work, I picked up a big stick and hit him with it." There was a brief pause. "I finally figured out what she was trying to tell me," he said, half to the officer and half to himself.

"Are the police here to arrest my uncle?" I asked.

Mrs. Weaver looked at me curiously. "No, dear. They're here to arrest the Johnson boy."

"Why?"

"Your uncle is pressing charges against him for assault."

"What! That's crazy. Reds was protecting me from him." First I pointed to myself, and then I pointed towards my uncle's cottage. "If anyone should be pressing charges for assault, it should be me. Against my uncle!" Those were brave words. Truth on fire.

"I thought maybe you would have something to say about that. Just go downstairs and tell your side of the story. Set things straight."

I hesitated. If I told what had happened to me, it would change the way people thought about me. But I knew I was hanging on to an identity that no longer fit me. I had outgrown it like one of Wendy's summer dresses. "I can't."

"Yes, honey child, you can. You need to give the secret away to another to look after it. Give yourself some time to heal. You can't do it alone." She nodded toward the stairs. "Go on, now. You can do it. "I'll be waiting for you on the third floor. Come see me when you're done."

I nodded and limped as best as I could downstairs. I reached the bottom, and Wendy, Julie, and Reds were there waiting for me.

Julie walked over and hugged me. I whispered in her ear, smelling her citrus shampoo. "I just wanted to be more like you."

"Hey, remember that you're an original. Remember the moments that define you . . . good and bad. That's what makes you special. Besides, you're the bravest girl I know. Actually, I wish I was more like you."

I stepped back to look into her blue eyes. Emotions clogged up my throat and I couldn't swallow or talk, so I just smiled sadly and nodded at her.

"Just keep your head above water, New Girl, and everything will be okay." She said my nickname like it was a badge of honor.

I sniffed back tears as I watched her and Wendy walk out the front door.

Reds walked over to me and hugged me.

I hugged back. I inhaled, taking in a deep breath of him. He smelled like pine trees, mud, and fish. He smelled like the river. Our river.

The police officer shuffled and I heard his handcuffs jingle. I let go of Reds, but he didn't want to let go of me. I reached into my pocket and pulled out the flattened penny my mom had given me. I rubbed it between my finger and thumb one last time, feeling its smoothness. I handed it to him. "Here. Penny for your thoughts."

His eyes got watery. "I take back what I said before."

"What?"

"You know, about the penny." He held it up in front of his face.

I gave him a quizzical look.

"It's not worthless. It's worth *everything*." He smiled a sad smile, turned, and went to the door.

Our emotions were tangled together and I wanted to cry too. We were like evergreen trees in winter, laden with snow, bent over with the weight of what we knew.

The door closed behind him, and I felt empty. Scared. I was too young to carry around this amount of pain, of guilt and of shame. I needed to let the sparrows fly away.

I limped over to the police officer, gathering my bravery. I cleared my throat. At first, I tried to push the words up, but they tasted like mud. I cleared my throat again, this time I could feel my throat open and the words float up like sparrows. "I have something to tell you."

It happened. I would forever be something different because of it. But it wouldn't kill me like I thought it would. As the words spilled effortlessly from me, I knew I would always keep talking. I would tell anyone who would listen to me to TELL SOMEONE if something bad happens. The truth was muddy and dirty and sharp. But it would no longer cut my throat if I spoke.

After the officer wrote down my story, he said he would file the report and let us know what would happen next.

I waited until the officer shut the door behind him before I climbed the three flights of stairs. Mrs. Weaver was sitting in a chair facing the north side of the camp, looking out the window toward the river.

The ceiling was slanted on the right side and on the left were two rocking chairs facing the window, which was the same shape as a stop sign. It was dark and cozy with lots of books. It was a perfect tiny library.

"I thought I might sit with you up here. I need—"

"No explanation needed, girl. This is where I come when things are too much for me."

I sat in the rocking chair next to her. I knew it was her husband's chair.

"I was watching last night. I saw what your uncle was doing to you on the path. And you weren't the first, honey. I remember your uncle years ago when he was in high school. He was skipping school with a girl about his age. I watched them on the path by the river and they just seemed like a young couple canoodling. I didn't pay too much mind. Then I heard the girl scream. I watched her struggle against his grip, and I knew something was wrong.

Luckily, I ran out and stopped him before he could do anything. I called the police, but they said it was my word against his. Of course he denied everything, and the girl had run off as soon as he let go of her. Since the police couldn't do anything, I did the next best thing. I called the truant officer and they caught him. He got a suspension from school and all related activities."

I gasped. I cried. I couldn't speak.

"I see everything from up here." She motioned with her hand for me to look out the window.

I got up from my chair and stood in front of the window. It was breathtaking. I could see the entire camp, including the river.

"You can see everything." She paused. "Or you can see nothing at all."

I looked long and hard, silently staring out the window. I didn't have to see anything at all, but I opened my mind's eye and saw everything.

I saw my mother running toward me. I saw a child become a woman. I saw the sparkling stars on the river and I saw dandelions in the sky. I saw everything.

I stayed on top of the world with Mrs. Weaver for as long as possible, but I knew I couldn't avoid the inevitable. I was just waiting as long as I could, waiting for my mother to come fly me away home.

After receiving her BA in English from Virginia Common-
wealth University, life swept Tina Sears away from writing.
She worked as an Evidence Photographer for the FBI, a
Medical Photographer for a major teaching hospital and
a Ballroom Dance Instructor. But it was during her time as
contributing writer for The Fredericksburg Times that led
her back to her passion for writing. She received an MFA in
Creative Writing from Southern New Hampshire University.
She lives with her wife in Virginia.